ARTHUR
CHRISTMAS
THE NOVEL

Adapted by
JUSTINE & **RON FONTES**

STERLING CHILDREN'S BOOKS
New York

STERLING CHILDREN'S BOOKS
New York

An Imprint of Sterling Publishing
387 Park Avenue South
New York, NY 10016

STERLING CHILDREN'S BOOKS and the distinctive Sterling Children's Books logo
are trademarks of Sterling Publishing Co., Inc.

TM & © 2011 Sony Pictures Animation Inc.
All rights reserved.

ISBN 978-1-4027-9242-7 (paperback)

Distributed in Canada by Sterling Publishing
c/o Canadian Manda Group, 165 Dufferin Street
Toronto, Ontario, Canada M6K 3H6
Distributed in the United Kingdom by GMC Distribution Services
Castle Place, 166 High Street, Lewes, East Sussex, England BN7 1XU
Distributed in Australia by Capricorn Link (Australia) Pty. Ltd.
P.O. Box 704, Windsor, NSW 2756, Australia

For information about custom editions, special sales, and premium
and corporate purchases, please contact Sterling Special Sales at
800-805-5489 or specialsales@sterlingpublishing.com.

Manufactured in Canada
Lot #:
2 4 6 8 10 9 7 5 3 1
09/11

www.sterlingpublishing.com/kids

SIX-YEAR-OLD GWEN HINES was having doubts about Santa Claus, but she still wanted to believe.

On November 25, Gwen wrote a letter to Santa. Then she put on her jacket, her woolly hat, and her gloves, and ran out of her house in the quiet village of Trelew, in the country of Cornwall, England.

Gwen trotted down Mimosa Avenue to the mailbox. She stretched up on her tiptoes to reach the slot and carefully slid in the envelope addressed to:

SANTA CLAUS

THE NORTH POLE

Three days later, Gwen's letter arrived at the North Pole's Mail Department, along with millions of others addressed the same way. It traveled down a hall made of shining ice and past a series of office doors until it reached one labeled Mail Agent 3776.

Behind that door sat a lanky young man named Arthur. Arthur believed in Santa completely! He knew for certain that Santa was real, because Santa Claus was his father, just like his grandfather had once been Santa and his great-grandfather before that.

Huge stacks of letters contributed to the cozy clutter of Arthur's office, which also contained an impressive collection of Santa memorabilia. Strings of stamps from all over the world hung in loops like paper chains, decorating the crowded shelves. Even though he lived at the North Pole all year, Arthur was a bit of a Christmas nerd!

Arthur ran one hand through his messy hair as he read Gwen's letter. Though he read hundreds of such letters each day during the North Pole's busy season, Arthur never tired of them. Each child felt special and important to him; each letter commanded the youngest Claus's complete attention.

Gwen's letter began . . .

Dear Santa,

My friend doesn't believe in you, because to get around the world in one night, you'd have to go so fast it would make you and the sleigh and the reindeer all burn up. I think you are real. But how do you do it?

Arthur smiled, glad that Gwen had not let her friend's skepticism spoil her belief. He glanced from her letter to the unopened collector's edition reindeer slippers at the heart of his "shrine" to Santa Claus. Arthur believed in Santa with all his heart. He was glad his position in the Mail Department gave him the chance to nurture that same faith in others.

He returned his attention to Gwen's words . . .

For Christmas, I would love a pink Twinkle Bike with training wheels. But PLEASE don't bring it if it makes you and the reindeer burn.

Love,

Gwen Hines

23 Mimosa Avenue

Trelew, Cornwall, England

Gwen had attached a postcard of her hometown. On the back, she had made a crayon drawing showing her on a pink bicycle waving to a red-clad Santa Claus—on fire!

Arthur grinned. Gwen's concern for Santa's safety was very sweet. But she need not fear. Santa Claus could perform his annual miracle without risk to himself or the reindeer. The rosy-cheeked, twinkly-eyed man in the picture on the wall of Arthur's shrine could do anything—at least that's what Arthur fervently believed. So he wrote:

Dear Gwen,

Thank you for your letter and brilliant picture. Your request for a pink Twinkle Bike will be passed on to Santa. Yes, do believe in Santa. He is real, and he's the greatest man ever. And he can get around the world to every child without a single reindeer being incinerat—

Arthur stopped himself, and changed the word to *hurt*, concluding, *By the time the sun comes up on Christmas Day, he'll get to you, too! Using his . . . special magic.*

By Christmas Eve, millions of similar letters had been processed, gifts made or acquired, wrapped, tagged, and prepared for delivery in an operation more efficient and better organized than any undertaking known to humanity.

While cities slept under a blanket of stars, a nearly invisible shadow slid through the sky at tremendous speed. No sleigh for Santa any more—this was the S-1, an incredible, huge, mile-wide "sleigh ship," designed by Santa's older son, Steve. When the craft stopped, millions of hatches opened, and tiny figures swooped down on wires. Quicker and quieter than ninjas, this army of elves "invaded" every corner of the world, racing over dark streets, across rooftops, and even down the occasional chimney, to bring the correct toy to every child on the planet!

At 11:56 p.m., the S-1 had reached the town of Aarhus in Eastern Denmark. An elf named Carlos Connor spoke into his high-tech headset. "First Field Elf Battalion—set!"

A large figure wearing a red suit trimmed with white, emerged from the sleigh and replied, "Ho, ho, ho!" He was, of course, Santa Claus!

Andrew Marino, the elf standing nearest Santa, relayed this go-ahead command. "That's a Ho, ho, ho, Aarhus."

All over the Danish city, tiny watches suddenly glowed green as millions of elves sprang into action.

Carlos Connor spoke urgently into his headset. "Field elves! Jingle! Jingle! Jingle! Drop time: 18.14 seconds per household!"

Elves on every roof near Connor disabled burglar alarms and obscured security cameras. They expertly disconnected wires and decoded keypads. They tossed snow "grenades" that kept cameras from tracking their lightning-fast entrances and exits.

Like fearless mountain climbers, elves rappelled down tall towers. They slid through windows and air vents, over fire escapes and through skylights.

They swung from strings of lights over plastic reindeer and Styrofoam Santas, before skiing down roofs. Some used sucker-padded shoes to scale the sides of skyscrapers. The elves moved with the agility of gymnasts and the stealth of thieves.

Santa, on the other hand, struggled to maneuver his bulk down a short ladder held steady by two loyal elves. His labored breathing echoed in his frostbitten ears. On this, his seventieth Christmas, the current Claus wondered, "Am I getting too old for this? No, of course not!" Santa had a job to do— and the night's amazing mission was nearing its successful conclusion!

A team of elves made their way down a suburban street. Before alley cats could open their mouths to meow, an elf turned his gun to "CAT" and dispensed a barrage of tuna-flavored treats. Similarly, a dog-food grenade silenced a guard dog.

Every type of gift, no matter how large, cumbersome, or noisy, reached its proper destination beautifully wrapped and perfectly assembled. Though most houses no longer had chimneys, the elves found their way in, deposited the right gifts, and left without waking so much as a mouse.

Disguised as doctors, they delivered to every sick child in hospitals. Prepared for every possible problem, the elves even had a peanut gun to shoot into the beak of a parrot that squawked loudly.

They had special gadgets designed to bite the carrots children left out "For Rudolph" and the other reindeer. They used hoses to suck up the pudding left "For Santa" into containers strapped to their tiny backs.

An electronic scanner measured the Nice/Naughty percentage of each child, allowing the stocking-filler gun to dispense the proper amount of small toys, chocolate coins, and candy canes.

The elves efficiently slid every kind of gift under tree after tree, and stuffed stockings with lightning speed, all without knocking over one knickknack or card.

Incredibly, within the 18.14 seconds, all the elf teams emerged from their targets with their gifts successfully dispatched. Carlos Connor reported proudly to the camouflaged craft, "Stand by S-1! Aarhus is Merry. Aarhus is Merry!"

The elves grabbed the wires and shot back up on them to the waiting ship, as air jets in the soles of their tiny shoes erased their footprints from the snow below. No trace of their visit was left behind. As each trio of elves ascended, they saluted Santa before disappearing into the craft.

As it flew through a dense cloud between stops, the S-1 momentarily dropped its starry camouflage, revealing it to be a giant red spaceship, the most modern craft on Earth!

Commanding it from Mission Control, Steve Claus said, "North Pole to S-1, you have weather fluctuation, update camouflage."

One of the elves assigned to maintaining the craft's disguise replied, "Roger that, Control."

Cameras all over the S-1's surface clicked to life. Suddenly the huge craft was cloaked in images of the land beneath. It was making itself invisible by projecting its surroundings onto itself! "Hull projection optimized," the elf reported.

The helmsman, Chris Tankenson, reported, "Denmark cleared."

Other elves echoed excitedly, "Denmark cleared." "That's an X-12 on Denmark."

Determined to keep them focused on the best delivery operation, Steve said, "OK, next drop Flensburg, minus 12.4 seconds."

AS THE SPEEDING S-1 approached Germany, one of the elf specialists jammed the nation's Air Defense Radar on five different frequencies. A computerized voice from the North Pole Mission Control played through the S-1's monitors. It reminded the elf, "Four hours to mission deadline."

The elf's tiny, sensitive ears twitched at yet another sound, a tentative knock on the door and a muffled voice saying, "Hello . . . ?"

The elf knew that voice and pressed a button that caused the door to SWISH open and a red carpet to unroll for Santa Claus. His jolly demeanor and big red suit made the man instantly recognizable. At his approach, all the elves present quickly saluted. Santa shuffled inside, muttering, "Sorry . . . Forgot the pin code." He could not get used to all the passwords and codes required by Steve's new technology. But Santa still wanted to stay on top of the mission. "So, how're we, uh . . ."

The eager helmsman answered Santa's question before he could finish. "Just crossed into Germany, sir."

"Germany." Santa stifled a belch. "Aren't we doing well?"

"Certainly are, sir," Tankenson replied.

Santa almost belched again, and then apologized. "Umf . . . sorry . . . one too many . . . mince pies." His belly was bloated with all the treats combined with the stress of the season. He patted his pockets, looking for the antacid tablets Mrs. Claus always made sure were there.

Tankenson filled the awkward silence. "Great achievement, sir." Then he added, "Looking forward to retirement?"

Santa hadn't heard him over his own chewing. He had found the roll of chalky tablets and had already popped two into his mouth.

The computerized voice recited, "Ten seconds to Flensburg."

Santa yawned. White chunks of dissolving tablets dotted his tongue. "Maintain current . . . um . . . Carry on all!"

The computer went on, "Update national protocol. Delete rice pudding and carrot. Germans leave out a shoe on the front step for Santa to fill. Repeat: Shoe on front step."

The same voice echoed in the S-1's giant Dispatch Deck where millions of gifts traveled along a maze of conveyor belts. As each gift passed through a control point, a scanner read the tiny barcode on its tag. On the computer screen of the nearby checker elf, the number would appear, ticking off the delivery for the child assigned that particular barcode.

Past the scanner, teams of delivery elves huddled beside their hatches, waiting for other elves to attach a gift to their back. The room resonated with numbers, followed by the constantly repeated phrase, "Gift secured!"

Dispatch Chief Carlos Connor kept his crew briskly focused. "You! MOVE!" he shouted to a dreamy elf named Tardy Baynham.

"What happened to peace and goodwill to all men, Sarge?" Tardy wondered.

Connor grumbled. "It don't say nothing about elves, soldier. GO! GO! GO!"

Over the speaker, Steve commanded, "Engage rooftops!"

Another elf hooked Tardy to his wire and pushed him out of the huge ship. Wind whistled through Tardy's pointy little ears as he suddenly sped toward the ground.

Live images of his speedy descent reached Mission Control at the North Pole, monitored on a giant screen by the dashing Steve Claus, Arthur's older brother. All the support elves admired their brilliant, handsome, dynamic leader, especially Steve's assistant, Peter. Everything about Steve, from his neat, white Christmas tree–shaped goatee to his trim, muscular physique inspired adoration in the fawning elf—even the way Steve sipped his espresso.

"Commencing Flensburg drop," the computer's voice reported.

Steve commanded. "S-1, hold drop altitude. This is Germany, Father. They drive on the right, national dish is sausage" He looked at the big screen showing Santa landing on a rooftop.

He clapped his hands to rally the elves. "OK, let's show them, people. Operation Santa Claus is coming to town."

Steve's deep, authoritative voice echoed off the walls of the huge, secret space dug into a glacier. His bright blue eyes—younger, clearer versions of his father's—reflected the giant banks of screens displaying the weather, S-1's status, plus military and civilian transmissions from all over the world.

Teams of elves worked in front of each screen. One watched the Santa Monitoring Station, which kept track of the big, jolly man's heart rate, cookie consumption, and Ho, ho, ho's per second.

Numbers flashed across the other screens, each representing a present delivered. Elves clicked buttons and recited "Drop Complete!" Each drop registered on an enormous counter.

Thousands of support elves sat on a giant ice-stepped platform in front of their monitors. At the top of the stairs stood a huge ice sculpture of Santa beneath big brass letters proclaiming the North Pole's sacred motto: In Santa We Believe.

On a walkway near the icy ceiling, a door opened, and Arthur stepped out. In honor of the special occasion, the youngest Claus wore a bright green Christmas sweater, and he had finally opened the package containing the silly, singing reindeer slippers. The furry slippers felt warm and cozy, though Arthur could not see his feet over the tall stack of papers filling his gangly arms.

Not used to walking in plush slippers, he tripped on a slick step and his papers went flying. "Oops! Sorry!"

Support elves scurried to retrieve the scattered letters. Arthur knew each letter by the color of its crayoned scrawl, and its sweet contents.

A busy elf named David wondered, "What are you doing, Arthur?"

"I have to get Maria Costa down to Steve," the younger Claus brother explained. But as he reached for the letter in question, it floated away from him. When Arthur tried to grab Maria's letter, he suddenly became painfully aware of the dizzying drop beneath the elevated walkway. He leaned back, wincing with vertigo and nausea, fighting the intense desire to drop down flat to hug the floor.

With a windy *WHOOSH*, an open elevator platform with no handrails soared up to become level with the walkway. An elf stepped off, holding out Maria's letter. "Is this yours, Arthur?"

"Oh thanks, Kenneth!" Arthur gratefully accepted the page. Then he added, "Merry Christmas!"

David stepped onto the elevator platform. "Need a ride?" He joked, knowing that Arthur was scared of heights.

Kenneth, David, and other nearby elves giggled. Arthur declined, "No, no thanks. Uh, I'm not very good with going fast and being high up and . . ."

Arthur winced again as the platform sped off. Images on the multiple screens showing elves plummeting to Earth made him feel even queasier.

Far below Arthur, Steve strode across Mission Control's floor with Peter at his heels. Arthur was in awe of Steve's confidence, clarity, and drive. His brother seemed the very picture of competence as he punched the buttons on his HoPad, the latest in high-tech devices.

Steve commanded, "Buckle down, people!" Then he turned to his assistant and demanded, "Peter, update!"

Meanwhile, Steve's clumsy brother couldn't even climb down a flight of stairs without creating chaos. Arthur apologized as he tripped past busy elves working hard at their screens.

These support elves communicated with the delivery elves in the field, issuing important information like, "Seventh step from the top had a squeak last year." Whenever elves encountered a problem they couldn't solve, they turned to Steve who always had a quick, decisive answer.

Peter gushed with admiration. "What a night, sir!" Then he added more softly. "Your father's seventieth. Out with the old Santa in with the new, eh?!"

Steve smiled modestly, making him look even more attractive. "Let's focus on now, eh, Peter?" Then he told everyone, "Support teams, prep Poland!"

Arthur muttered to himself, "Wow! They call Dad *Swienty Mikolaj* there, you know." He asked the elves, "Do you know how many names there are for Santa worldwide?" When no one answered, the young Santa buff exclaimed, "Thirty-two!"

Arthur was so excited that he slipped on the ice. Trying to recover his balance, he snagged a wire that knocked over three elves! When Arthur tried to pick them up, he only made things worse.

"Ow!" one exclaimed.

"That's my ear!" the second protested.

"Ugh," the third moaned.

Arthur felt miserable about hurting the little fellows. "Oh! Oh dear! I'm terribly sorry! Are you alright?"

Steve ignored everything, except his vital mission. "Special forces! How are we doing at the White House?"

"Eleven minutes to presidential child one, sir," replied the elf in charge of that sector.

Steve glanced from the elf to the bank of screens showing the White House, Kremlin, Buckingham Palace, and the homes of other world leaders.

"Two hours, forty minutes to Mission Deadline," the computer reported.

Meanwhile, Arthur tried to untangle himself from the cable and the angry elves. But his new slippers slipped out from under him and he tumbled down the ice stairs toward Steve. The handsome older Claus could not hide his impatience—nor did he try.

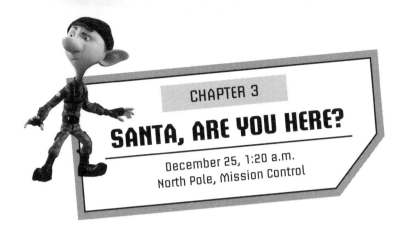

ARTHUR WAS EMBARRASSED that he tripped over the elves. "Sorry, Steve! It's my slippers on the ice!" He held up one of the reindeer slippers. It blinked brightly and played a brief burst of "We Wish You a Merry Christmas."

Steve was not amused. So Arthur quickly came to the point of his visit. "Maria Costa! She asked for a Pocket-Puppy, but she really wants the blue one with the long ears, 'cause it looks like her auntie's dog Biffo that ran away. I remembered 'cause she sent a photo of Biffo, see?"

Steve struggled to keep his temper with his infuriating younger brother. Couldn't he understand how busy Steve was? His deep voice held a note of warning. "Arthur . . ."

Oblivious that he was bothering Steve, Arthur persisted, "Did she get the blue one?"

Peter consulted his HoPad. "Child CG786K. She lives in Greece, sir! That was six countries ago."

"Oh. I just want Christmas to be perfect for every kid!" Arthur explained. Then he suddenly noticed the image on the Santa Monitor screen. "Hey, there's Dad!" Arthur stared adoringly and shouted as if his distant father could hear him. "SANTA!"

Arthur waved and saluted, which sent his letters flying all over the icy floor again. Support elves scrambled to retrieve them.

Steve put a hand on Arthur's bony shoulder. "Little bro . . . It's great to have you around. You bring a genuine aura of seasonal . . . positivity. But, could you not be in Mission Control? At all. For the rest of the night?"

Shocked, disappointed, and embarrassed, Arthur blinked. He spoke quietly. "Oh. Um . . . yeah. Of course." He forced a smile. His feet carried him slowly out of the huge room.

"They should put him somewhere out of harm's way," one elf said under his breath.

"Where? Like the South Pole?" Another elf replied.

Arthur tried not to notice their laughter.

The sudden blare of an alarm interrupted Arthur's humiliation. Red lights flashed as the alarm rang.

From Santa's personal field unit, Seamus Malone shouted in his thick Scottish accent, "WAKER! WE HAVE A WAKER! AND SANTA'S IN THERE!"

Arthur turned around to see what was happening just as Mission Control's automatic door shut him out.

The big screen showed a little boy sitting up in bed. The elves in the boy's room took immediate evasive action. One froze behind a curtain. Another flicked off the nightlight.

One climbed up a wall to hide on the ceiling while another hung on the door under the boy's bathrobe. Still another elf hung from the mobile above the child's bed.

"Santa? Are you here?" the sleepy boy asked.

Santa was indeed lying on the floor of the boy's room, having tripped on the child's skateboard. His head rested on a present. When he lifted his head, the package started to *MOO!*

Santa put his head back down and froze while Field Sergeant Andrew Marino used his Hoho to contact Mission Control.

Steve comforted the distressed Santa. "Hold on, Father." Then he barked to the support elves, "Intel, get me INTEL!"

All around Steve, elves sprang into action, summoning plans for the boy's house, details about the waker's gift, and anything else that might be helpful.

Peter assessed the situation. "Santa's head appears to be resting on some sort of 'Try Me' button, sir."

Elves gasped in horror.

"It's the Quack Quack Moo Activity Farm, sir. It features twelve separate animal sounds and sings 'Old McDonald Had a Farm' in six languages," added a thorough elf named Deborah.

Peter said, "The moment your father lifts his head there'll be ten seconds of constant mooing."

The computer added to the tense moment by reporting, "Sixty minutes to Mission Deadline."

Steve concluded, "Captain Marino, you're going to have to take out the batteries."

Deborah fretted, "But he'd have to get past the wrapping, the box, and fourteen twist ties anchoring it to the cardboard!"

Support elves also worried. "What if it goes off?"

"It's too noisy!"

"It'll wake the boy!"

Seamus Malone expressed everyone's deepest fear, "He'll see Santa!"

An even gloomier old Scottish elf moaned miserably, "Remember 1816! Santa was seen, and they tracked him home. He had to go into hiding . . . no Christmas for six years . . . the elves all alone!"

As fear threatened to escalate into pure panic, Steve commanded, "CALM, PEOPLE! It's not 1816 now!" Then he told Marino, "Your Hoho is equipped with state of the art electronic monitoring frequency sensor technology hacked directly from NATO's missile program. I want you to locate the batteries and perform a Level 3 gift-wrap incision. Go in through the robin."

One of Marino's men gently lowered earmuffs over the sleepy kid's ears while the sergeant scanned the box with his Hoho. The device showed a skeleton of the toy, with a flashing light indicating the location of the batteries.

Marino used a tiny scalpel to delicately cut around the cheery robin on the wrapping paper. He peeled it back and saw a twist tie holding the toy in place. So far so good!

With a shaking hand, Marino wiped his sweaty brow before unscrewing the battery compartment with a miniature screwdriver. Support elves watched their screens, fascinated by the delicate operation. One gift sorter on the S-1 Dispatch Deck froze with his coffee cup in mid-air.

Nearby in the Claus family's living quarters, an old man in pajamas grumbled at the same image on his TV set. He sat in an armchair with a blanket draped over his knobby knees. He grumbled, "Ha. Lot of fuss! I did *my* seventy missions without any of this malarkey!"

No one heard the old man because he was alone, except for the ancient, one-antlered reindeer snoozing in a basket at his feet. When the door opened with a blast of arctic air, the old man looked up.

Arthur hesitated in the open doorway. "Can I watch with you, Grandsanta?"

"Shut the door! Christmas berries, it's the North Pole!" the senior Claus, 136 years old, reminded his grandson.

Arthur shut the door and turned his attention to the TV, asking anxiously, "Is the kid still asleep? He mustn't see Santa. Dad would rather die than spoil it for him!"

Santa Claus XVII scoffed. "What if you do wake the odd nipper? A whack on the head with a sock full of sand and a dab of whisky on the lips—they don't remember in the morning! He, he, he . . ."

On the screen, a backup elf swung through the window on a wire to deliver a pair of long-nosed tweezers. Marino took the tweezers and started carefully lifting out the batteries.

Grandsanta continued griping. "What happened to going down the chimbley? Didn't do me any har . . ."

Before he could finish the word, a fit of coughing shook the old man's fragile shoulders, expelling a black cloud of dust. The reindeer woke with a start and tried to climb into his master's lap to lick him.

"Get off! Get off!" Grandsanta told Dasher.

Arthur tried to help, but he felt nervous around the reindeer, afraid it might bite or poke him with its antler. Arthur was anxious about a lot of things.

Just then, the door opened again and Mrs. Claus exclaimed, "Goodness!" She carried a tray of tea and mince pie.

"Down, boy! Basket!" she commanded, and Dasher instantly obeyed.

"Here you are, Grandsanta," Mrs. Claus went on. "I've made you a nice mince pie."

"I can't eat that. Gets in me teeth," the old man grumbled.

"Oh, dear," Mrs. Claus replied. "Now I have to finish the ones for the elves. There may be 2 million of them, but nobody gets left out while I'm Mrs. Claus." She opened the kitchen door, revealing millions of mince pies in various stages of completion. Then the busy woman returned to her work.

Arthur could not take his eyes off the TV. "Nearly there!"

Sergeant Marino held up the battery and sighed, "Clear!"

But lights flashed on and the wrapping paper began to rip.

"Oh no!" Arthur exclaimed.

In Mission Control, Deborah explained, "It's the detachable milkmaid!"

Another support elf added, "She's got her own power source!"

Deborah warned, "They've got five seconds until she starts singing!"

Support elves gasped with dread. Could Marino save Santa—or would the mission fail?!

The gift sorter who had been holding his coffee cup up couldn't take the tension any longer. Never taking his gaze off the screen, he slammed down the cup. The elf did not notice that the cup bumped a button, and behind him, an arm shifted on a conveyor belt, knocking one gift to the ground!

Deborah began the terrifying countdown to disaster, "4 . . . 3 . . . 2 . . ."

"Use your Hoho! Exit code 12! Code 12!" Steve shouted.

Through the wrapping paper dotted with red-breasted robins, the toy flashed and repeated two lines of a song over and over.

The tiny cameras mounted on the field elves' hats showed the frantic scene as they bundled Santa out the window and the little boy sat up in bed.

The boy opened his eyes and looked around, just as Santa's feet vanished behind a curtain. Two elves swung their flashlights across the curtains, like headlights. They also made sounds like the joyous voices and music of a loud party in a passing car.

The groggy child lay back down to sleep. "So it wasn't Santa after all . . ."

The elves in Mission Control heaved a collective sigh of relief. Steve commanded, "OK, GO! GO! GO! Revise Drop Time to 14 seconds! Let's pick this up!!"

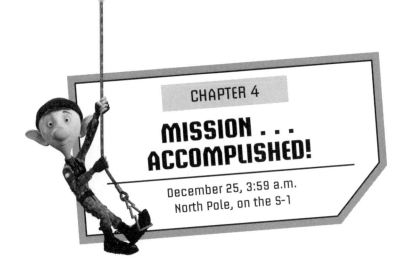

IN A WHOOSH, the S-1 was on its way, streaking invisibly through the night. Soon the great moment arrived. As the giant Mission Control counter clicked down with the final deliveries, joyous elves counted along: 3 . . . 2 . . . 1 . . .

"Mission complete," the North Pole computer reported robotically when the counter displayed all zeroes.

The elves cheered! They bumped their tiny fists, hugged, and passed out candy canes. Some even cried with relief and happiness.

Steve smiled with pride over of his vital contribution to this successful mission. Peter grinned, "This is just the start of the celebrations, eh, sir? I . . . got you a present."

Steve unwrapped his assistant's gift and found red silk boxer shorts embroidered with an S.

"Not S for *Steve*, sir," Peter explained with a sly wink. "S for *Santa*."

Steve may have felt almost as certain of his impending appointment as Peter. But he said, "Oh, I don't know about that. OK, let's bring them home."

After its amazing journey, the S-1 looked somewhat weather-beaten. But it slid gracefully between icebergs as it slipped into the arctic waters of the North Pole. The ship glided through the frigid sea under the ice to rise in the huge docking bay.

Masses of field elves swarmed the dock to meet the support elves who had accompanied Santa on his mission. Arthur's messy hair and skinny shoulders loomed about the bustling crowd as he worked his way closer to the S-1. He nearly jumped out of his skin when the ship suddenly released a loud cloud of steam.

Helmsman Tankenson teased, "Fancy a trip on the S-1, Arthur? It only goes 150,000 miles an hour."

The other elves nearby joined in the laughter as Arthur replied, "No, no . . . I'm happy in Letters, thanks! I see a bit of the world in my office, you know. Some of the stamps I get are amazing!"

BEEP! Arthur jumped again as a Gift-wrap Recycling Machine rumbled across the dock, gathering up loose paper. "Excuse me," said Bryony, the elf driving the noisy machine.

"Arthur gets travel sick on one of those, don't you, Arthur?" David teased. The elves around him snickered.

Bryony sped up the Recycler to scatter them.

Then suddenly a huge cheer rose up from the crowd as Santa emerged from the S-1. Hundreds of elves waved their tiny arms and exclaimed, "Santa's waving at me!"

Arthur waved, too, shouting, "Dad! Happy Christmas!"

Santa smiled and said, "Arthur! You too!"

Arthur held up his feet, "Look! Christmas slippers!"

Santa laughed, "Well done!" He turned and spotted his elder son, "Aah, there he is, Steve!"

When Arthur's brother and father shook hands, the elves cheered even louder. Arthur sighed. *Would Dad ever pat me on the back like that?*

Santa's black boots climbed the steps up to a podium. Flanked by his wife, sons, and father, Santa boomed, "Mission . . . accomplished!"

A million tiny hats suddenly danced through the air along with a vast cheer. Then the tired-but-jolly Santa went on, "Tonight we delivered two billion presents, on this my seventieth mission. My biggest year ever!"

His microphone squealed and Steve adjusted it. Santa nodded and said to Steve, "You know, sometimes I think I couldn't do it without you!"

Steve smiled graciously as Santa went on. "And there's my splendid wife, Margaret, who's stood by me all these years very ably doing all that . . . stuff women do when their husbands are at work. Marvelous!"

The old Scottish elf shouted, "Gaw bless Mrs. S. She's a good 'un!"

The snore behind him reminded Santa to add, "And uh . . . my father, of course, a great . . . um . . . support. Now . . . ."

Before Santa could go on, his wife coughed to remind him of the other person on the podium.

Santa stumbled, "Oh, and . . . er, Arthur, yes. Doing vital work in Maintenance, really vital . . ."

"No, dear. It's . . ." Mrs. Claus started to correct him.

Arthur chimed in, "I, um . . . work in Letters, Dad. I've been there two years. You moved me after I tripped over that plug and melted down the elf barracks."

A nearby elf recalled bitterly, "I lost everything in that flood!"

"Letters! Yes, of course," Santa said hastily. "Not Maintenance, no, no."

Santa resumed his speech, "Now, tonight's a big night!"

Behind the podium, Peter signaled to three elves: One poised to pop the cork off a sparkling juice bottle, a second waiting to unfurl a huge banner, and a third holding the rip cord to release a net full of balloons. "Stand by," Peter whispered with urgent excitement.

"I've had seventy wonderful years doing the best job in the world," Santa went on. "And, uh, I'm sure you all know what's coming . . ."

Peter took a deep breath. The trio of elves watched for his signal.

Santa concluded, "I can't wait for year seventy-one! Merry Christmas, everyone!"

Steve and Mrs. Claus blinked in surprise. Like Peter, they both had been sure Santa would announce his retirement. Peter's jaw dropped and his hand fell, too. So the three elves took this as the cue to pop the corks, set free the balloons, and unroll the giant CONGRATULATIONS STEVE banner.

Not bothering to read the banner or wonder why the balloons looked like his elder son, Santa assumed all the fuss was for him. After all, he was the big man at the North Pole!

Soon the huge docking bay was empty, except for the cleaning machine chugging across the littered floor, picking up the burst balloons and other scraps.

CHAPTER 5

WHO GETS TO BE . . . SANTA?

December 25, 4:43 a.m.
North Pole, Residential Quarters

IN THE CLAUS quarters, Arthur's honking laugh echoed as he joked, "What do you get if you eat Christmas decorations? Tinsilitis! Honk, honk, honk," the youngest Claus cracked himself up. But no one else joined in his laughter.

Steve sulked over his Hoho3000, a device that looked like a super high-tech cell phone, scanning for new job opportunities. Santa picked at his turkey dinner while Mrs. Claus fed Dasher. Then she tied Grandsanta's napkin around his scrawny neck like a baby's bib and took Dasher outside for a walk. Grandsanta grumbled, "Lookit Techno Tommy, he's tekksin' on his calkilator lookin' for another job, ha, ha!"

"It's a Handheld Operational and Homing Organizer, the Hoho3000," Steve corrected him.

Then he lied smoothly, "And I'm not job hunting. I'm enacting mission closure."

Steve hastily wiped the job listings off his Hoho screen and deleted several irate and potentially embarrassing e-mails from Peter.

But Grandsanta's teasing went on. "Oo, whoopee doo, aren't you the fancy Nancy? Don't matter what you come up with, Son. You may be next in line, but you'll never get to be Santa unless you knock 'em off!"

An awkward silence followed this remark. Then Arthur chirped, "Um . . . I've got you all a present. After all the hard work I wanted everyone to have fun for Christmas! Ta da!"

He pulled a box out from under his chair and displayed Christmas: The Board Game to his family. Arthur glanced at the happy family on the back of the bright box and the slogan: Fun for ALL the Family. Guaranteed Festive Cheer!

At that moment, the elf Bryony was sweeping the Dispatch Deck on the S-1. Because the S-1 was so big, Bryony rode the Gift-wrap Recycling Machine. She was almost done cleaning the deck when something jammed into the rotating brushes. Bryony climbed down to find the problem. Among a pile of wrapping paper scraps, there it was. She gasped in horror. A present had been missed!

❄   ❄   ❄

Meanwhile, the cranky Clauses seemed anything but festive. Before they could even start to play Arthur's game, the other three Claus men started fighting over the tiny silver Santa figure.

Grandsanta exclaimed, "I'm Santa!"

"No, *I'm* Santa!" Steve asserted. "You took the piece out of my hand!"

Santa said, "Well, I am *actually* Santa, so I rather think *I* should have it."

Steve replied, "Well, yes, you're the nonexecutive 'figurehead.'"

Santa seized on this. "Exactly! The figurehead."

"He means a fatty with a beard who fits the suit," Grandsanta spat bitterly.

Arthur tried desperately to make peace. "The other pieces are good, too! Or, I can make extra Santas for everyone."

"Why don't you be the candle, Steve?" Santa suggested. "All those bright ideas, eh?"

"Fine!" Steve exclaimed. "I'm the candle, Arthur's the turkey, and you, Father, are, of course, Santa. Grandsanta can be this charming relic." He handed Grandsanta a tiny sleigh. Then Steve rolled the dice.

"Relic? RELIC?" the old man shouted. "I did the whole Christmas in one of those, and I didn't need a trillion elves to help."

Steve sighed. He was so sick of having this same argument. "The world's a bit more complicated than in your day, Grandsanta, with about a billion more children. And we don't just fly about throwing lead-painted toys down chimneys."

With a burst of arctic air, Mrs. Claus came back inside. She banged the snow off her boots and tossed a small, smelly bag into the trash before taking Dasher off his leash. She unwound her scarf and approached the table.

Grandsanta rolled the dice. As his tiny sleigh landed on a certain square, Steve said, "That space sends you back to Lapland." He moved the sleigh back to START.

Grandsanta complained loudly. Then Mrs. Claus looked at her husband, who had somehow acquired a stack of tiny toy gifts without even taking a turn yet. "Where did you get those?" she asked.

Santa yawned. "Just moving things along. . . . Do I win?"

Grandsanta exclaimed, "Cheats, the pair of you!"

When Mrs. Claus took off her coat, Arthur reacted

in alarm to a huge claw rip down the back. "Mum! Are you OK?"

Mrs. Claus shrugged off the deadly danger. "Polar bear, dear. Big silly. Good job I did that online survival course, or it would've been one less for turkey next year."

Indifferent to his daughter-in-law's narrow escape, Grandsanta griped on, "Christmas has gone completely downhill. You're a postman with a spaceship!"

Steve sputtered, "My S-1 festivized the world at 1,860 times the speed of sound!"

Grandsanta huffed. "Christmas 1941. World War II. I did the whole thing with six reindeer and a drunken elf. Got shot at—twelve direct hits! Lost three reindeer—and still managed to do it all and bring home a buffalo for Christmas dinner."

Arthur had heard that story many times, but he never tired of it.

"I could still do it now!" Grandsanta shrieked. "Just gimme a go!"

Steve shrieked back, "In a heap of sticks?"

Santa chuckled, "Goodness me!"

It was Grandsanta's turn to sputter in outrage. "Heap of . . . Oh, it's funny is it?! Let me up and at 'em! I'll show you, Robbie the Robot!"

Grandsanta's arms flailed as he struggled to pull himself out of his chair. He knocked the game board over with his cane, scattering pieces all over the floor.

Mrs. Claus sighed. "Every Christmas, it's the same thing!"

BLEEP! Steve's pager suddenly pierced the air with its shrill, electronic whine. Steve scrambled to check his Hoho3000. The message he found shocked him so much, Steve gasped and ran into the hall.

Grandsanta called after him, "Oh yeah, run away now that you're losing."

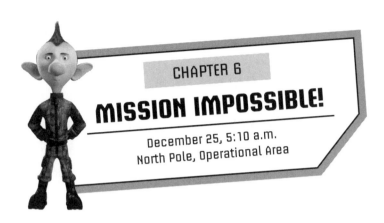

ARTHUR FOLLOWED, WONDERING what could have upset his brother so much. Was Steve still angry about the game—or their father's decision not to retire yet? Arthur pushed the little metal Santa into his brother's hand. "You keep this," Arthur said. "Then you can be Santa next time."

The two brothers stood in a hall lined with portraits of Santas through the centuries. Frame after frame filled with jolly, cherry-cheeked men, all the way to their father, followed by an empty space.

Arthur assured Steve, "It'll be you up there soon, I bet. You'll be great!"

Steve shivered in the draft from the open door and exclaimed in annoyance. "How many times, Arthur? It's the North Pole! Shut the doors!"

Arthur shrugged sheepishly. Mission Control was nearly empty.

Steve stared at his Hoho screen, his handsome face creased with concern.

"I secured the gift, sir. Gift secured!" Bryony the elf saluted proudly. Her free hand clutched a package that was obviously a small bicycle, despite its perfect wrapping. Peter stood beside her on the dock, looking exasperated with the enthusiastic elf.

Steve moaned, "It just can't be! The system is foolproof!"

Bryony did not know what to say. When not on cleaning detail, she was a gift wrapper. So she added some important good news. "Present wrapping is intact, sir!"

Peter ignored the zealous elf and agreed with his boss. "It must be an error."

Bryony gushed on about her exciting discovery. "I spotted the sticky tape glinting in the shadows, sir. I'm actually trained in wrapping, and I said to myself, 'Bryony, the wrapping looks okay, thank goodness, but that present should not be lying in the . . .'"

Steve interrupted impatiently. "Yes, yes, thank you."

Arthur, overhearing the conversation, looked over his brother's broad shoulder. He exclaimed, "Oh no! Did someone get the wrong present? That's awful! Whose is it?" He hated to think of any of the many children who believed in Santa being disappointed.

Peter scanned the gift's tag and reported, "47785BXK did NOT 'get the wrong present.'" He typed the child identifier number into his Hoho, then added, " . . . or . . . um, the right one."

Arthur gasped. "The child got . . . nothing? At all? No!" in his horror, he shouted, "A child's been MISSED?!"

Steve tried to calm his excitable brother. "Not necessarily." He still refused to believe his advanced, modern system could be flawed. But even as he spoke, the giant Gift's Delivered Counter clicked back from all zeroes to 000,000,001.

Arthur shouted even louder, "A CHILD'S BEEN MI . . ."

Steve interrupted, "Arthur! Do you want to wake the whole North Pole?"

Arthur agreed, "Good idea!" He ran to the door and shouted the shocking truth even louder. "A CHILD'S BEEN MISSED!"

"ARTHUR!" Steve shouted in exasperation. But it was too late.

Santa came down the hall, yawning. "Everything alright?"

Steve admitted, "There's been . . . a glitch."

Arthur marveled at his brother's dismissive tone. "A GLITCH? WE'VE MISSED A CHILD!" Each time he shouted it, the tragedy seemed even more unthinkable!

Santa was surprised. "Really? Dear, oh, dear," Santa muttered. He hoped this would not involve any personal blame—or having to go out in the cold again. He added, "How on Earth did you manage that, Steven?"

Steve was irritated. How dare his father grab the credit and evade the blame. "Me?! I thought this was *your* mission!"

"Oh, no, no, no, this is your department," Santa replied hastily.

Arthur felt as if he was having a nightmare. Who cared who was responsible? The important thing was making sure the child received a gift before morning. He demanded, "What are we going to do?"

Santa blustered. "We must . . . um . . . we must . . . what must we do, Steven? Do I need to get my boots back on?" Just the thought of this made the tired, old man yawn.

"Absolutely not!" Steve declared, to Santa's relief. "A loss of delivery is deeply regrettable. But the mission was a success!"

Arthur could not believe his big ears. "But we CAN'T leave out a child on Christmas!"

Peter tapped more keys on his Hoho.

Steve sighed, as the data reached his screen. "Sunrise at destination is 7:39 a.m. There's no way to get there on time. Except, of course, in the S-1. But it just traveled seven million miles! It needs months of engineering checks! We could damage it!" Realizing the S-1 didn't mean as much to everyone else as it did to him, Steve added, "And risk the lives of the elves!"

Bryony told Santa, "I'll go, sir! Bryony Shelfley, Wrapping Operative Grade Three, sir!" Her tiny heart stirred with excitement at the thought that she might be able to serve on this vital, dangerous mission.

"I wasn't called up for field duty this year. I served out the mission in Gift-wrap Support, wrapped 264,000 presents in three days, sir! If you want that bike delivered in a full state of enwrapment, then I'm your elf!"

"No one is going!" Steve stated.

Santa started to object, "But this child . . ."

". . . is a margin of error of 0.000000001514384 percent." Steve flashed perfect teeth in a perfect smile. "WOW. I mean, hello? Where's the champagne? That's incredible! My department has delivered the most outstanding Christmas ever!"

Santa felt uncertain and even more tired than before. "Oh, uh . . . well done us!" he agreed with his clever, older son.

Arthur felt unmoved by the impressive percentage. "But the kid got no present."

Numbers confused Santa, but he knew this was not good. Sensing his father's indecision, Steve quickly added, "It's a statistical anomaly."

Arthur countered, "The child's been good all year!"

Steve spoke smoothly, "Arthur, no one feels this more than I do. But Christmas is not a time for emotion. We'll get 44785BXK a present within the *window* of Christmas. We can messenger the item to arrive within five days."

Arthur shrieked, "That'll ruin the magic!"

Steve chuckled at his silly younger brother. "If there was any way to make the drop tonight . . . but it can't be done."

Arthur turned to their father, full of faith that Santa would make things right. But the old man just yawned and said, "I won't sleep easy after this, Arthur. But there it is. It can't be done."

Steve patted Arthur's bony shoulders. "Go to bed, little bro. Merry Christmas."

Then Steve and Santa walked away, leaving Arthur and Bryony to stare in stunned silence at the giant counter's lonely "1" beneath the golden motto, "In Santa We Believe."

Arthur raced to the dock and snatched the gift from Bryony. As he ran off with it under his arm, the concerned elf shouted after him, "You're compromising the wrapping!"

RIP! Bryony cringed as the paper snagged on a door, but Arthur was gone. He had to know the identity of 47785BXK.

Finally, he found the letter and postcard stamped with that unlucky designation. Arthur read the letter and recognized the postcard from Gwen Hines of 23 Mimosa Avenue, Trelew, Cornwall, England. He instantly remembered the little girl whose friend thought Santa's mission was "impossible," the good little girl who wanted the "pink Twinkle Bike."

Arthur looked at the clock near his shrine to Santa Claus. 5:24 a.m. Could Gwen's friend be correct? Was delivering her gift really "impossible"? Arthur's thin shoulders slumped with abject defeat.

At that moment, Steve stared at a red designer suit neatly trimmed with white. This would have been his Santa suit. But . . . he hung it back in the closet and switched off his light.

Meanwhile, Santa hung up his well-worn suit and

wondered, "This figurehead thingy . . . I'm not just a fatty with a suit, am I?"

"Of course not, dear," Mrs. Claus assured him mechanically. How could she tell her husband that his eyes had lost that special twinkle?

Santa fretted on, "And retire . . . what would I do all day?"

"Well, we could spend more time together, maybe take up gardening," Mrs. Claus suggested. "It's a little tricky at the North Pole, but there's a lot you can grow in containers. And there's Steve . . . and Arthur . . ."

Santa sighed. "Arthur. Oh, dear. What a puzzle." Would his second son ever be good at anything?

Santa said, "I'm still very much up for the job, you know." But his Ho, ho, ho faded out into a huge yawn. "Night, dear," Santa muttered, just before he became lost in snores.

IN THE DARKNESS, tiny lights flickered in the flashing eyes of Arthur's reindeer slippers. Too miserable to sleep, Arthur stared at Gwen's letter by these blinking lights.

"It can't be . . . it just can't be . . ." Arthur muttered over and over again, until finally he slammed his head on his desk, dislodging the shelf full of Santa knickknacks.

"What's all this kadoodle, young man?"

Arthur turned; he was surprised to see Grandsanta and Dasher in the doorway. He waved Gwen's letter and explained, "It's this little girl: She's been missed!"

Grandsanta exclaimed, "Ha! So much for your brother's fancy-pants technology!"

"No, Steve and Dad racked their brains, but it's impossible!" replied Arthur.

Grandsanta was skeptical. "Is it now? Missed a child! Dear, oh, dear, sends shivers down me shins."

Arthur glanced at the clock again and imagined Gwen. "In two hours she's going to wake up, tear downstairs, search under the tree, and . . ." He couldn't bear it. "But there's NOTHING THERE! She won't understand. She'll think she's the one kid in the world who Santa doesn't care about."

Grandsanta was only half-listening. His wrinkled face glowed with excitement as his aged brain hatched a plan. "D'you know, Arthur. There *is* a way!"

But the young man felt lost in melancholy. "It's impossible!"

Grandsanta scoffed. "They used to say it was impossible to teach women to read!" Then he added slyly, "Follow me."

The old man led his grandson down a dark hall toward the Abandoned Toy Depot in a dusty, unused section of the vast North Pole complex. Arthur's slippers blinked, and his flashlight beam cast a lonely cone of light in the blackness. Dasher whined nervously as they walked past rusty shelves under a sign that read Dolls and Toys.

Grandsanta unlocked a large door that creaked slowly open. Arthur's flashlight beam discovered a familiar shape coated in shiny red paint. On a brass plate, he read three letters that spelled the name *EVE*. The old man switched on a single bare light bulb that hung above the antique sleigh.

Arthur gasped in wonder and disbelief. "The sleigh! The actual sleigh!"

Grandsanta sighed. "Hello, Evie."

"I thought it was scrapped years ago!" Arthur exclaimed.

Grandsanta grinned mischievously. "So did everyone else."

"Can I . . . ?" Arthur's fingers reached eagerly toward the legendary object, longing to touch the smooth wood. "Icelandic birch, Arctic balsa, built in 1845, able to reach 50,000 mph at a height of 40,000 feet!" Arthur's stomach lurched just at the thought of such speed and height.

Grandsanta wheezed as he struggled to lift a large, rusty drum. Arthur hurried to help him wrestle it onto the sleigh.

The peeling label read Potash of Carboniloroxy Amilocitrate. Arthur recognized the formula for the sleigh's special fuel. "Oh! Magic dust!"

Grandsanta nodded. "Mined from the Aurora Borealis."

Arthur felt confused. "But . . . she doesn't still . . . go?"

Grandsanta grinned. His cloudy old eyes twinkled as he threw open another door. Beyond it, through a fine net of cobwebs, Arthur saw stables where eight reindeer shuffled in their hay like restless horses.

"Not just a hobby," Grandsanta said. "Great-great-grandchildren of the original eight!" Then he took a brass horn off a hook. He blew into it, but no sound emerged, just a dead mouse. Grandsanta's wrinkled old cheeks puffed as he blew the horn again. This time Arthur and the reindeer heard a weak-yet-hauntingly-beautiful note.

"Wow!" Arthur whispered reverently.

Grandsanta called out, "Dancer! Prancer!" He struggled with his faded memory. "Er . . . What are the others called? Bambi? John! You there, with the white ear! And you and you and not you, you bag of fleas!"

Arthur felt uncomfortable as the reindeer responded to the old man's command. "Uh . . . oh . . . er . . . I'm not really good with big animals."

Grandsanta dismissed his fear. "Piffle!"

Arthur laughed nervously.

Grandsanta said, "Don't get bit. They can smell fear. Let's hitch 'em up."

Suddenly Arthur was up to his elbows in antlers. "Ah, uh . . . excuse me . . ." He told his grandfather, "You can go to Gwen, on the old sleigh with the reindeer and the magic dust and everything. It's a miracle!"

"You're coming, too, lad."

Arthur froze. The journey combined all his worst fears. "Me?! On THAT? Up THERE? Pulled by THEM? No, no, no way!"

Grandsanta protested. "I'm 136! I can't do it on me own, I need an elf!"

Arthur objected. "I can't fly a sleigh! I can't even ride a bike without training wheels!" His mind raced for a solution. "I know. Let's wake Steve. He'll . . ."

Grandsanta shook his head. "What if he stops us? Gwen's forgotten."

Arthur felt touched by his grandfather's concern. "You really care!"

"Of course, I do!" Grandsanta agreed hastily. "I was Santa, too!" His old eyes flickered over the young man, calculating exactly how to persuade him. "Think of your dad, lying awake, chewing his beard off worrying over this girl. Don't you want to *help* for once? Make him *proud*?"

Arthur was frozen. "I can't! I just . . . I can't. No . . . NO! I CAN'T!"

Nevertheless, a few minutes later, Arthur found himself huddled in Eve's foot well, clutching Gwen's bike. As the ancient elevator lifted Eve out of the complex into the open air, Arthur shook like the faded flags marking the North Pole and flapping in the arctic wind.

The eight beautiful young reindeer were now harnessed to the sleigh. As he held their reins, Grandsanta's chest puffed with pride beneath his mothball-scented, old Santa suit.

Dasher sat on the sleigh's back seat, his nose excitedly sniffing the icy wind. Grandsanta looked back and asked his terrified passenger, "Ready?"

Arthur's buckteeth chattered with cold and fear, as he replied, "NO!"

But Grandsanta flicked the reins anyway, and the eight reindeer trotted forward.

Arthur felt the sleigh start to move and begged, "You *promise* not to go too fast?"

Grandsanta's response did not reassure the young man. "Woohoo!"

"Or high! Or bumpy, I get travel sick!" Arthur reminded the old man. "And I'm allergic to snow!"

"Ye baubles!" Grandsanta exclaimed. "And you a son of Santa?"

As the sleigh picked up speed, it vibrated violently and loudly, like a washing machine with an unbalanced load. Grandsanta's dentures rattled wildly.

"Wait!" Arthur shouted, suddenly realizing he

wasn't wearing appropriate footgear. "My Christmas slippers!"

But it was too late. The sleigh was on its way—and with only two hours to reach Trelew before sunrise.

Grandsanta pulled a brass lever and a sparkly cloud of magic dust rained down over the reindeer. Instantly, their hooves left the ground as the deer floated into the air.

"Dash! DASH! DAAAAASHHH!" Grandsanta cried, just as Arthur screamed, "STOP! STOP! STOOOOOP!"

The reindeer obeyed the red-suited man with the reins, and their hearts beat with glee as they fulfilled their destiny.

Grandsanta looked back at the North Pole and punched the air in defiant triumph. "See? Who's Santa *now*?!" The sleigh climbed higher, toward a glorious moon, leaving a trail of glittering dust. "HO, HO, HO! WHOOHOO!!" the old man crooned, just before Eve suddenly plunged down, lurching and shaking. The young reindeer bucked wildly, pulling in all different directions.

Arthur wailed into the wind, "AAAAAH! PUT ME DOWN!"

Grandsanta roared with laughter. "What's the matter, boy?"

Arthur gasped for breath. "I'm . . . having a . . . heart attack . . ."

Suddenly, Arthur was sick over the side of the sleigh.

Grandsanta laughed and nodded at the reindeer. "Whoops! They've never flown before! Just gotta break 'em in! Now, now . . ."

Grandsanta's hands steadied the reins, and his withered lips pursed to produce a strange, silvery whistle. "COME AWAY! DASH AWAY!" he commanded.

The skill of driving a flying sleigh came back to him, never lost, like riding a bike. The young reindeer fell into line. Their leaping strides assumed an easy rhythm.

Dasher sat up and bleated with joy. Arthur found the courage to peek above the rim of the sleigh at the flying deer and the starry sky.

Grandsanta encouraged him, "Look, Arthur, all those stars. We're one of 'em now—a shooting star!"

As the old man steered, momentum threw Arthur back onto the seat. A small object fell from the dashboard: a little nodding reindeer toy.

Grandsanta's eyes stared back over the years as he recalled, "Stuck that there for your dad when he was a boy."

Arthur tried to picture his large father as a small boy. "Dad . . . sat *here?*"

Grandsanta nodded. "So did I. And my dad before me and his dad before him. Every young heir to the Pole gets took out by his father. Right back to Saint Nick!"

Wind puffed out the mothball-scented suit, helping Arthur see the Santa his grandfather had once been. The old man recalled, "We Clauses used to be the only men in the world who could fly."

He waved at the world below. "It was a gift, from Santa to his eldest son, this great big ball wrapped in oceans and mountains. I remember the look on your father's face when he saw it."

Arthur's curiosity grew. He peeped past the flying reindeer to gaze at the beautiful world of moonlit snow, shimmering sea, towering icebergs, and the glowing green wonder of the Aurora Borealis!

As Eve traveled farther south, the Northern Lights faded, and ice gave way to ocean. Grandsanta swooped closer to the water. Naturally drawn to the magic, narwhals leaped beside the sleigh. Arthur whooped with delight! "Fish with horns!"

Grandsanta smiled and suggested, "Want to help me make a snowman?" Before Arthur could answer, he winked, then steered Eve right into a cloud bank!

"No! Not y . . . ," Arthur protested too late.

Steam blasted from a pipe as the sleigh swooped in crazy patterns. Arthur screamed, until Eve emerged from the clouds.

When the young man looked back, his yell became a laugh. The clouds had been sculpted into a giant snowman!

Grandsanta laughed, too. Arthur stared into the old man's twinkling eyes and saw someone who was artistic, romantic . . . Santa!

Arthur released his white-knuckled grip on Eve's side just long enough to punch the air and cry, "Woohoo!"

CHAPTER 8

SKY-SCRATCHERS AND A STOWAWAY

December 25, 5:42 a.m.
Current Location Unknown
Time until Sunrise: 2 hours 2 minutes

GRANDSANTA CHUCKLED, AND then he pulled out a brass sextant and a thick square of folded parchment.

Arthur looked back at the fading snowman and wondered, "Could Dad do that?! Did he make a snowman for Steve?"

The twinkle fled from Grandsanta's eyes as the crabby old man returned. "Robot Roy? Ha! He took one look at Evie, said she was aerodynamically challenged and violated 11 safety codes!" Grandsanta shook his head. "Heck of a five-year-old he was. The next Santa and he's never even sat in a sleigh!"

Arthur's eyes fell on the folded parchment. His voice choked with awe as he asked, "Is that?"

Grandsanta nodded. "The map of the Clauses. Used every Christmas night in history!" The old man lifted the sextant to align it with the stars. "Whatever your brother says, Arthur, it's the same old world!"

But something terrifying appeared from the clouds! A big, saucer-shaped object!

"WWWAAAHHH!" Arthur and Grandsanta screamed in unison.

Grandsanta swerved at the last moment. Eve spiraled down.

"Wh . . . what is it?!" Arthur gasped.

Grandsanta tightened his grip on the reins and replied, "No idea! I've never seen it before!"

As Eve broke out beneath the cloud, her passengers found themselves in a maze of skyscrapers! The big saucer was the tip of a skyscraper.

Arthur exclaimed, "It's a CITY!"

Grandsanta tsk-tisked and grumbled. "A new 'un. They're always putting these things up."

Arthur winced as the old man narrowly missed the glass and steel towers. Eve avoided a building, but clipped a satellite dish, smacked into a sign and snagged several cables.

"Ahhh!" Arthur's fear returned in full force.

Grandsanta said, "I remember the first time I ran into Chicago! Ha, ha, ha, I'll never forget . . ."

Arthur's fear grew even more urgent. He

interrupted. "*Chicago* wasn't on the map?! Whoa! Watch out for the . . ."

He ducked just in time to avoid bashing his brains on a clock tower. Grandsanta turned the map around. Arthur cringed as the old man took his eyes off their obstacle course and said, "No, you draw it in, don't you? Here, see . . ."

Arthur panicked. "Whoa! Um. Just, um . . ."

Grandsanta continued to stare at the ancient parchment. "Oh no, that's Peking . . ."

"Um . . . ahead, there's a . . ."

Grandsanta steered the sleigh just in time to avoid smashing right into a glass building. Arthur saw a couple inside the skyscraper kissing under the mistletoe. "Uh oh! They can see us!" he fretted.

"Well, pull the camouflage lever!" Grandsanta commanded. Then he pulled out a quill pen and muttered, "Better draw in a few of these 'sky-scratchers' . . ."

Arthur grabbed the lever. Painted wooden panels flapped down around the sleigh, disguising it as an old steam train. Unfortunately, they also completely obscured the view!

Grandsanta cried, "Not that one! Can't see a thing!"

The "steam train" plummeted to the ground,

smashing the camouflage panels into splinters.

"Woohoo!" Grandsanta exclaimed, before returning to writing on the map. "So what'd they call this place?"

Arthur looked up at the electronic sign just as the rising sleigh smacked into it: "Toronto Welcomes Careful Drivers. Your speed: 16,024 mph."

Grandsanta wrote, "Tor . . . on . . . to."

Arthur exclaimed, "Toronto's in CANADA!"

This did not surprise the old man. "The Santas always come through Canada! Nobody lives here!"

But everywhere Arthur looked was crowded with buildings full of windows, streets, cars, stores, and more "sky-scratchers."

The sleigh bounced into a giant inflatable Santa decorating the top of a tall building. The young reindeers' antlers became tangled in garlands of fake elves, pulling open a front panel on the sleigh.

Grandsanta frantically swiped at the garland, but suddenly came face to face with a real elf!

"Ahhh!" Bryony exclaimed.

"Ye baubles, an elf!" the startled old man shouted.

"Bryony Shelfley, Wrapping Operative Grade 3!" She carried the kit of a field wrapping elf and offered, "There's a small trauma to your gift wrap, sir. But I can fix it!"

Grandsanta scowled, "A stowaway!"

"I can wrap anything, sir! With three bits of sticky tape! Three!" Bryony added with her usual enthusiasm.

"Good. Wrap yourself a parachute," the old man quipped as he tossed Bryony out of the sleigh.

The elf screamed! And so did Arthur. "Grandsanta!"

Bryony simultaneously activated both of her shoulder-mounted tape guns and attached herself to the speeding sleigh. Still, she swung wildly off Eve's back, like a doll tied to a bicycle.

Arthur rushed over to help and pulled the elf back into the sleigh.

Grandsanta seemed completely indifferent to Bryony's brush with doom. He folded the map and reported, "Toronto, present and correct."

Bryony pointed out the front of the sleigh. "Not quite, sir. You've lost a reindeer."

In the confusion of their rooftop crash, Grandsanta and Arthur had not noticed the harness snap, releasing one of the reindeer. The bewildered animal freed itself from beneath the deflated Santa and emerged in a Toronto city park.

❅   ❅   ❅

Meanwhile, back at the North Pole, Steve woke to the *BEEP BEEP* of his Hoho3000. He groggily pressed a button and Peter appeared on the screen. "Hello?" Steve asked.

"Bryony Shelfley," Peter said, "never returned to her barracks, sir. Security tracked her to Sector 19. And . . . we think Arthur was here."

Steve wondered why Security suspected his brother was involved. "Arthur?"

"Someone left a door open," Peter explained.

Steve groaned as Peter stepped back to reveal the old sleigh barn, with its doors open to the exit tunnel. Behind him a security elf lay pinned to the floor by a polar bear. Behind them, seals and birds flapped.

"But the old sleigh barn was sealed decades ago, after that terrible night Grandsanta sneaked out and . . . Thank goodness, he's too old to cause any more trouble," Steve muttered.

❄   ❄   ❄

"Bash it with a brick!" Grandsanta urged Arthur, "Go on!"

Eve was stopped at a tractor dealership in Dayton, Idaho: 1,660 miles in the wrong direction and with only an hour and a half left till dawn in Trelew, England.

"Grab its antlers and tug!" the old man shouted, as Arthur struggled to free the metal reindeer from the logo on the remote building's roof.

"It's stuck!" Arthur exclaimed. "Ow! The snow . . . Sorry, it's my allergy."

Grandsanta sighed, wishing for the strength of his youth. "Come on, lad! You're as useless as a cheese chopstick!"

Then suddenly, the metal deer broke free of the sign. "Got it!" Arthur gasped. But then he saw its other side: It was hollow, only half a deer!

Grandsanta shrugged. "It'll have to do. Pass it down to me."

Arthur felt confused. "But . . . don't we need a whole one? You know, to balance the sleigh?"

"Oh, it won't balance the sleigh," Grandsanta replied. "If anything, it'll slow us down."

Bryony tried to get their attention. But the two Clauses ignored the elf.

"So why are we taking it?" Arthur wondered.

"It's for Gwen," Grandsanta explained. "Eight beautiful reindeer. That's what she's dreaming of—the jingly bells, the sleigh on the roof, and Santa coming down the chimbley, ho, ho . . ." A fit of coughing interrupted his laugh.

Arthur still felt uncertain. "Yeah . . . but . . ."

Grandsanta ranted, "That's what the kids want, not some spaceship! We're giving her the star treatment."

Bryony interrupted their discussion with urgent news. "We have a Waker, sir. With a gun!"

BANG! A shot shattered the still air. Bob, the tractor dealer, stood outside his house in his pajamas, rifle raised to aim at the roof. The logo-deer clattered to the ground, knocking over the ladder, leaving Arthur stranded.

Ignoring his grandson's predicament, Grandsanta hobbled to the sleigh, where the panicked reindeer skittered.

Arthur screamed, "Grandsanta!"

Bob walked slowly closer to the roof, his gun still aimed at the mysterious thieves. "Who . . . who's there?" he called out.

Backlit by the remains of the sign, with his big feet, skinny limbs and tight hood, Arthur looked like an alien. His words only added to Bob's confusion, "Um . . . Peace and goodwill! We are on a vital mission . . ."

Bob's flashlight beam played over Arthur's feet. Thanks to the reindeer slippers, they looked large and furry. Then the beam found Arthur's bucktoothed face, barely visible inside his hood, and blotchy from cold and his snow allergy.

Arthur went on, "Our . . . uh . . . craft has to travel round the world in less than an hour!"

Terrified beyond reason, Bob fired again. *BANG!*

Tangled in strings of Christmas lights from the sign, the deer took off, pulling the sleigh in a circle, trailing flashing twinkle lights.

Grandsanta released a cloud of magic dust, and the sleigh rose up like a blinking, spinning UFO!

Bob's jaw dropped in shock as the "alien" grabbed onto the back of the UFO and flew away, shouting, "Sorry we can't pay. Where I come from, we don't have money!"

Stunned, Bob watched the glittering, glowing craft until it disappeared into a cloud.

ARTHUR STARED DOWN past the metal deer dangling from Eve's harness to the Atlantic Ocean far below. He had never seen anything as big as this ocean. "Do you think we should stop and ask someone for directions?"

"Pishywibble!" Grandsanta replied. "We're nearly there! See, I take the North Star there as a fixed point . . ." He pointed out a bright spot adding, "Then I plot my bearings from . . . um . . ."

Grandsanta's voice trailed off as the "North Star" moved swiftly across the sky!

"That's a plane, sir," Bryony said.

"Insubordination!" Grandsanta shouted angrily. "I'll have you harpooned, elf!"

Arthur tugged at his parka. "I thought it would be

chillier near England." He glanced at a palm-fringed island below.

"Uh, globular warming," Grandsanta muttered. Then he exclaimed, "Ha! Land ahoy! Told you!"

The sleigh swooped down toward the coast. But as they neared land, Arthur marveled at the waving green grass, balmy breeze, and lilting cicadas' song.

"Wow, England," Arthur remarked as the sleigh settled down on the lush grass. A large, exotic bug crawled over his shoulder.

Grandsanta looked around and finally conceded "Maybe we pulled to the right a bit; we're a reindeer short. France!" He climbed down and hobbled off the sleigh, shouting, "BONJOUR! OU EST LE BOULANGERIE?"

"BBBRRRRRMPHHH!" An elephant trumpeted loudly.

Arthur was puzzled. "They have elephants in France?"

Grandsanta did not yet want to admit his mistake, so he fibbed. "The odd stray. They breed in the drains."

Then he consulted his ancient parchment and pushed aside a scraggly bush. Beyond it stretched a vast plain full of giraffes, elephants, meerkats, and other African wild life. Grandsanta clung to his lie. "Paris Zoo!"

He walked forward, with Arthur and Bryony on his heels. But even Arthur was having trouble believing the old man. "We landed in the zoo?"

"Um . . . if we did . . . then this is the lion enclosure!" Bryony observed nervously.

A pride of lions had begun to circle them!

"They won't eat me—I'm Santa!" Grandsanta declared. Then he tried to command the beasts. "Lie down!"

The nearest lion growled. The deep, ferocious rumble shook the old man's confidence. He stepped back and said, "Um . . . right . . . call the keeper!"

Arthur grabbed the map and unfolded it, trying to figure out where they were. His eyes widened as he read the antique and alarming entries. "How old is this? Constantinople? Atlantis? 'Here be CANNIBALS?'"

"You got to watch out for cannibals," Grandsanta declared.

As the hungry lions closed in on the travelers, Arthur was becoming frantic. "This isn't France, is it?"

"Course, it is!"

"Technically, it's known as Africa," Bryony began with the continent, and then became more specific. "The Serengeti National Park, in the country of Tanzania."

Grandsanta scoffed, "Rubbish! How can you possibly be sure?!"

"The GPS on my Hoho, sir!" Bryony explained. "It cross references seven satellites to pinpoint our location to within three feet . . ."

Her voice trailed off as Grandsanta pushed Bryony in front of him and offered her to the nearest lion. "Take her! Take the elf!"

"A GPS!" Arthur exclaimed. "Why didn't you say?!"

"I'm a wrapping elf. I don't navigate. I wrap," Bryony stated. She waved her Hoho. "I use it to store pictures of bows."

The lions slinked closer, opening their jaws to reveal deadly fangs.

Grandsanta quivered. "Help! I'm too young to die! Arthur!"

The young man was still processing their situation. "She's right. This is Africa! I've seen it on a stamp. You brought us to AFRICA! And we'll all be eaten, and we'll never get to Gwen!"

Arthur stared at Grandsanta, who suddenly looked like a scared, lost, little old man who begged pathetically, "Fight them! Save Santa! DO something! Arthur!!!!!"

But Arthur had never been faced with a life-ordeath responsibility before. What could he possibly do against a pride of lions?

❄   ❄   ❄

Meanwhile, at the North Pole, Steve was searching for a way to contact Arthur and Grandsanta. He called in Ernie, the head of Polar Communications. Ernie was the oldest elf ever. He wore pajamas adorned with medals, wheezing as he slowly set up a cobwebby contraption.

"Can we hurry this?" Steve said. He was getting impatient.

"Oh, you can't rush the Signalator. Got to play 'er gentle." Ernie continued to set up the dusty, old machine. The Signalator looked like an ancient typewriter. It was massive and had plenty of strange buttons and levers.

Ernie shoved an old wire into a socket. A shock buzzed through his body, causing his hair to stand up. The Signalator hummed to life. Colorful signal flags popped up, and Ernie, very pleased with himself, looked to Steve.

"So, what do you wish to say?"

❄   ❄   ❄

Back in Africa, Arthur didn't know how to handle the pride of lions coming toward him. Suddenly, without any thought at all, Arthur turned on his musical, electronic reindeer slippers and started singing along. "Silent Night, Holy Night . . ."

The sound surprised the lions. They had never heard a meal sing before. Neither had they ever seen reindeer slippers with flashing eyes.

The slippers and their terrified owner continued, "All is calm . . . All is bright . . ."

Arthur turned to Bryony and Grandsanta and shrugged. "I realize this is mental, but it's all that I know . . ."

Bryony and Grandsanta might have thought Arthur insane, but the lions were not attacking! Their round, yellow eyes seemed hypnotized by the blinking lights. And their large furry ears swiveled in response to the soothing song.

Arthur cooed, "It's Christmas, nice kitties. So please let us go . . ."

One by one, the mesmerized lions lay down! Grandsanta and Bryony joined in the song. So the three sang with Arthur's slippers, "Sleep in heavenly peace . . ."

Soon the whole pride settled down quietly around them. A magical moment of Christmas peace prevailed on the African plain. Slowly, carefully, and still singing, Arthur, Bryony, and Grandsanta made their way back to the sleigh.

". . . Sleep in heavenly peace."

Then just when it seemed they would be safely on their way, a loud *CLANG* shattered the calm. Tiny flags popped up on Eve's dashboard: a message on the old Signalator.

The three travelers jumped into the sleigh just as the startled lions resumed their attack!

"Dash! DASH!" Grandsanta commanded, as one lion swiped at the sleigh's Signalator.

Just as flags flapped and the claxon *CLANGED* on Eve, corresponding flags wiggled on Ernie's device at the Pole.

"Something's coming through!" he reported to Steve and Peter excitedly.

"What does it say?!" Steve demanded.

Unfortunately, Grandsanta wasn't working his Signalator. The lion's paw pushed at it wildly. Ernie scratched his head, but recited dutifully, "Chimney full of cocoa. Send robins."

Grandsanta swung his cane at the lion batting at the flag-waving device. "No!" he screamed at the naughty cat. "That Signalator is Christmas history, you mangy moron!"

Another lion snatched at Gwen's gift. Arthur pulled it away just in time, but the beast's claws tore at the pretty paper.

Like a miniature ninja, Bryony sprang into action. "HIIYYAAA!" she screamed. "Only children get to tear the wrapping!"

In a flash, she taped together the lion's paws. He stumbled off, as the elf explained to Arthur, "XD3 Automatic Sticky Tape Dispensers!"

Grandsanta shouted at another lion. "Get off! Get off it!"

"Laser-guided scissors . . . ," Bryony announced as she aimed the light at another lion, temporarily blinding it. The beast quickly retreated.

"Shoulder-mounted gift-wrap!" Bryony went on as she wrapped a third lion's head.

"There's no time for a bow!" Arthur exclaimed.

But Bryony could not abandon her training. "There's always time for a bow."

The lions didn't think so. They continued to attack, as Bryony frantically pushed buttons on Eve's dashboard.

One button caused an old-fashioned camera to pop up. Its flash momentarily startled a lion, but then the lion smashed the camera with a huge, powerful paw.

"Not MY CAMERA!" Grandsanta moaned.

Finally, the sleigh managed to get off the ground—only to crash into a grove of trees. Two more reindeer broke free of the harness, galloping across the plain to join a herd of antelope.

Arthur rolled the drum of magic dust to the edge of the sleigh and tipped it out over the remaining reindeer.

The sleigh flew safely away! But the wind caught the dust and carried the magic sparkles down to the lions, giraffes, zebras, and elephants, which soon floated above the savannah like huge, live balloons.

CHAPTER 10

TROUBLE IN TRELEW

December 25, 6:18 a.m.
1,368 Miles from Trelew

AT THIS AMAZING display, Arthur and Bryony burst out laughing. But Grandsanta wailed in misery. His beloved sleigh and his ancient map had both been badly torn by tree branches and savage claws.

"Look what they've done to my Evie!" the old man moaned. "And the map!"

"It's OK. We've got this," Arthur assured him. Then he typed into Bryony's Hoho, "Look . . . Mimosa Avenue . . . Trelew . . ."

After a few seconds of satellite contact and some quick calculations, Steve's recorded voice recited robotically over the Hoho, "Proceed to the highlighted route."

Grandsanta shook his head. "What's the point?

Look at us! And my camera, totally banjaxed. How do I get my picture now?"

"What picture?" Arthur asked.

"The sleigh on the roof, the eight beautiful reindeer, and Santa-me! Getting down the chimbley!" Grandsanta replied. "That's what I wanted 'em to see! *They* missed the kid, but *I* got there! My way!"

Arthur looked at his grandfather, deeply disillusioned. The horrible truth became clear. His heart sank faster than a sleigh without magic dust. "That's why you came," Arthur stated. "Not for Gwen."

Steve's recorded voice on the Hoho interrupted, "1,368 miles . . . then slight left."

Arthur felt too disappointed to speak. What could he say anyway? The important thing was to get Gwen her gift. So the sleigh sped through the night, silent except for the jingling bells of the harness and the whistling wind.

As they neared the coast, Steve's recorded voice announced, "Descend 1,000 feet."

They approached a town with a sign that said, "TRELEW."

Steve's recorded voice concluded, "You're at your destination."

Arthur and Bryony cheered. "Yaaaay!! We did it!"

Grandsanta sulked. "Whoop doo."

Steve's electronic voice droned on Bryony's Hoho. "In 100 yards, turn left . . . straight again . . . left again . . . turn right. You are at your client's dwelling."

Grandsanta struggled to steady the damaged sleigh. Eve bumped to a rough landing in an alley. A chunk of wood fell off.

Arthur leaped out, hugging the ground in joyous relief. "We made it! I survived!" he gushed, before kissing the ground. "I'll walk home! I'll get a boat! But I am never getting back in that crazy flying deathtrap ever again!"

BANG! The bike landed at his feet, kicked off the sleigh by Grandsanta. "Go on. Get it over. I want my bed," the old man grumbled.

Arthur did not understand. "You're not coming? You have to deliver the present. You've got your special coat on."

"You're our Santa," Bryony added.

But Grandsanta didn't care. "I said me and Evie could get here and we did. The rest is just elf-work."

Arthur scratched his head. "It doesn't matter how we got here. The sleigh on the roof, the jingle bells, the eight reindeer—Gwen would never have seen that."

He picked up the bike and stalked away. Bryony

followed him, leaving Grandsanta alone in his battered sleigh.

After a brief walk, they reached Number 23. Arthur's heart fluttered with excitement. Inside a child waited for Santa. He whispered, "I wish dad could see this. It would take such a load off his mind."

Focused on the mission, Bryony asked, "So what are your orders?"

Arthur looked blank.

Bryony sighed. "You're a Claus. You give the orders."

"Do I?" Arthur fumbled. "Oh . . . um . . . I'm just happy being an elf, really. You know, just . . . just part of it all!"

Bryony rolled her eyes in exasperation. "Do you want to order me to go through the cat door?"

That made sense to Arthur, so he agreed. "Oh. Um, yes! That's a great idea!"

The elf squeezed through the small opening, and then peeped out through the mail slot. "Do you want to tell me to let you in?"

"Brilliant," Arthur agreed gratefully. "Thank you, Bryony."

Locks rattled. Then the door opened and . . . an alarm began to *BEEP BEEP BEEP!*

Bryony looked at Arthur, who nodded. The

resourceful elf climbed up to the alarm box and with lightning speed wrapped it thickly with bright paper.

Beep beep beep! The now-muffled alarm whispered.

Arthur and Bryony crept farther into the house, toward the Christmas tree. Arthur's eyes grew wide with awe at its twinkling beauty and the excitement of the moment.

"Is this your first time?" Bryony wondered.

Arthur nodded, and the elf gently took his hand and led him forward toward the pile of presents. In the center, both saw a small bicycle, neatly wrapped in North Pole paper, with a tag that read "De: Santa."

Arthur sank to his knees in horror. How could there already be a gift from Santa? And why did the tag read "De" instead of "From"?

His wide eyes took in other clues to their location. This was not England any more than the Serengeti had been a zoo in France!

Before Arthur could form a question, the wrapping paper muffling the alarm shook loose and the alarm resumed its full volume *BEEP BEEP BEEP!*

WO-WO-WO-WOOF! The alarm woke a small dog that dashed into the room. The dog leaped on one of Arthur's furry slippers, embracing it passionately.

"He likes those slippers even more than you do," Bryony observed.

Arthur struggled out of a back window, and Bryony slammed it closed on their escape. The dog pressed against the glass, eyes wet.

Arthur looked down at his slipper, then opened the window and gave it to the love-struck little pooch. "Happy Christmas," he said. The dog's tail wagged wildly as its tiny paws closed around its prize.

As the travelers dashed down the street, Bryony looked around and asked, "When you put the address into the Hoho, what did you see?"

"A list of Trelews," Arthur recalled. "I just clicked on the first one . . ."

At the same moment, both Bryony and Arthur read a billboard: *Vota Alealde Domenguez, Para una mejor Trelew!*

Bryony exclaimed, "We're in the wrong Trelew!"

Sirens sounded from every direction at once, as police responded to the alarm at 23 Mimosa Avenue in Trelew, Mexico—7,425 miles from Trelew, England.

When the two reached the sleigh in the alley, Grandsanta pointed up at helicopters. "They've been watching us! They've seen Evie!"

Bryony grabbed the Hoho and tuned it to the latest news. A TV reporter announced, "Governments tonight are waking to news of a UFO traveling around the globe at incredible speed. Now suspected to be in

Mexico, the clearest sighting of the UFO was at this tractor dealership in Idaho."

Bob recalled his "close encounter" with horror. "It had eyes on its feet and a little pointy head! It asked me for a sign!"

The reporter went on. "And from the trail of destruction left in Toronto, these beings do NOT appear to be friendly."

At the North Pole's Mission Control, Steve watched the same report on his Hoho while surrounded by sleepy support elves.

As Peter searched the Internet, he, Steve, and the elves, realized that every nation on Earth was tracking the flying sleigh. There was even news footage of the floating African animals!

A Tanzanian reporter concluded unhappily, "The herd is now in Mozambique's airspace, threatening the fragile peace between the two nations."

Steve's stomach churned. "Two billion items delivered, and we didn't leave a footprint in the snow. And now . . ." However would he explain this mess to Santa?!

All around Steve, elves reported additional disasters. An Internet technology elf named Doug moaned, "Sir, we have 80 percent data loss."

Another said, "Sir, there's a polar bear on level six."

A third wondered, "Why is Arthur out there?"

Ernie, the old elf still trying to raise the sleigh on his Signalator, blurted out, "Santa missed a nipper, number 47785BXK."

Word began to spread through the North Pole's massive elf population that "a nipper" had been missed, and Arthur had gone to make the delivery.

Just then, Doug exclaimed, "Sir, we've got something! Bryony Shelfley's Hoho!"

∗　　　∗　　　∗

At that moment, Bryony stared at Arthur, who sat aboard the battered sleigh. He grabbed her tape guns and taped himself firmly to Eve's seat, stating boldly, "We can still get there! We just have to go faster . . . higher!"

Bryony admired his determination. "Ooh, you've changed your tune."

Suddenly another siren shrieked, sending Grandsanta clambering over the back seat. The frightened reindeer trotted out of the alley.

"I'm not going anywhere!" Grandsanta cried hysterically. He pulled the heavy blanket over his head to hide. "I'm not here!"

"Grandsanta come out!" Arthur called. But the old man was busy reliving his worst trauma.

"Leave me alone!" his muffled voice begged from

beneath the blanket. "It's 1962 all over again! I took Evie out for a spin. It was the Cuban Missile Crisis. I nearly started World War III!"

Arthur regretted taping himself to the seat. "Aaaah! Help! I'm stuck, my hands!" he screamed in frustration.

"Hold still," Bryony said as she whipped out her laser-guided scissors to cut him free, as the driverless sleigh careened down the road, reins flailing, jolting Bryony's scissors so the beam came within an inch of Arthur's eye! Another reindeer shook free and galloped away!

"Oh no!" Arthur exclaimed. "Fencer! Mincer! Come back!"

But there was no time to pursue the runaway deer. Police cars were converging on the sleigh, which was right out on the street in plain sight! Bryony pumped magic dust to help the sleigh lift off!

Still without a driver, Eve wove wildly through the sky. "Aaaaaah! Grandsanta get up here!" Arthur yelled.

Finally free of the tape, Arthur yanked the old man to the front of the sleigh.

"My new hip!" Grandsanta complained, though certainly seemed spry enough as he jumped down into the foot well.

"Please, listen, I'll read you Gwen's letter," Arthur pleaded.

Grandsanta shook his head. "Stone deaf. I'm 136."

But even the old "deaf" man heard something ringing. "What's that?"

Bryony stared at her flashing Hoho. "It's Steve!"

"Steve!" Arthur exclaimed, hoping his big brother could help them get out of this mess!

"Tell him I'm not here!" Grandsanta cried.

Bryony pressed the "answer" button on her Hoho and dutifully reported, "Grandsanta says he's not here."

Steve replied, "Hi! I'm looking for a missing relic."

DESPITE GRANDSANTA'S ATTEMPT at denial, Steve could clearly see the old man through Bryony's Hoho screen. Realizing this, Grandsanta changed his approach, trying instead to blame Arthur. "It was him! Frosty the Madman, he forced me to come!" He turned to Bryony and added, "Elf, back me up, if you want a career."

Arthur couldn't believe his big ears. "*I* forced *you*?"

"You see? Look!" Grandsanta said, pointing to the reins in Arthur's hand.

Steve knew better than to believe the wily old man. "What did you want, Grandsanta? Let me guess, hmm . . . a picture of you in the sleigh delivering the gift, to show me how it's *really* done?"

Grandsanta stuffed away the camera guiltily and lied, "No!"

Steve went on, "You know the picture they'll have tomorrow? You led away in handcuffs! The Santa who was seen by everybody on Earth, the Santa who ruined Christmas!"

"Ruined it!" Peter echoed.

Grandsanta grabbed the reins away from Arthur. "We'll fix this, Steve! We'll be back home in a wobble of a reindeer's buttocks, and Eve can go back in mothballs, you can forget she ever existed."

Arthur took back the reins. "You can't just go home! What about Gwen?"

"Gwen!" Steve exclaimed. "For that you'd threaten my whole operation?"

"Our glorious future of absolute perfection!" Peter added.

Realizing his ambitious assistant wasn't helping his cause, Steve said, "Get me an espresso, Peter."

"But it'll ruin Gwen's Christmas if Santa doesn't come," Arthur explained.

"He's not normal, Steve." Grandsanta grabbed for the reins. "Jingle this and silent that, he's obsessed! We'll come quietly!"

Once again, Arthur took back the reins. "Steve, you said if there was any way to get there, you would! Well, this is it! Look! The old sleigh is perfect!"

The image of Eve that the Hoho sent looked so far

from perfect that even Arthur had to admit, "Oh . . . well, anyway, it goes really fast even with bits missing. And we've got quite a few reindeer left . . . and if I'm sick again I can be sick in a bag!"

"I'll wrap him one!" Bryony promised.

Then Arthur begged his brother. "Steve, please."

Support elf Sarah Wilko chimed in, "We can help them, sir!"

"No one missed, sir!" the elf named Deborah added.

"All correct presents present and correct, sir!" another elf agreed.

All around Steve, elves sprang into action, punching in 47785BXK to put satellite images of Gwen's house on the big screen.

Arthur urged, "If you help us, Steve, we can do it!"

Everyone in Mission Control and on the Hoho screen stared at Steve. Then an over-eager elf named Thomas Jack piped up, saying just the wrong thing. "Grandsanta and Arthur would be the heroes of the night, sir!"

Peter dropped the espresso cup.

Steve argued, "Come home now! The whole Gwen thing, it's emotional thinking, Arthur. If we all just gave in to Christmas spirit, there'd be chaos!"

Grandsanta grabbed the reins. "We're on our way, Steve!"

But Arthur grabbed back the reins, even though Santa refused to let go. The skinny young man was surprisingly strong, but so was his aged adversary.

Arthur cried, "No! Santa will want us to get to Gwen! Ask him, please!"

Steve paused for a moment, and then smiled wryly. "Arthur, this is Dad we're talking about. He went to bed! Santa's just a part he plays. It's a suit. He's not interested."

Every cell in Arthur's body rebelled against this horrible idea. "You're wrong! He's lying awake worrying his beard off about Gwen!"

Steve pressed the big red *SANTA* button on the nearest phone. Arthur expected his father to pick up on the first ring, or maybe his mother. Instead, after several rings, the answering machine clicked on.

Santa's jolly, recorded voice began, "Ho, ho, ho, getting some shut-eye, please do not disturb um . . . 'til December 26 . . . Is that it, dear?"

Mrs. Claus's recorded voice replied to Santa, "Yes, Malcolm. Press the red but . . ."

The machine *BLEEPED*.

Arthur's heart sank. He shook his head furiously, refusing to accept the awful truth. "No! Santa's the most caring man in the world!"

"So, why are you here and not him?" Bryony wondered.

Arthur turned to Bryony and stared blankly. He had no answer to that. He dropped the reins just as Grandsanta yanked hard.

The sleigh suddenly flipped upside down. The Hoho flew up in the air.

Steve called, "Arthur?!"

But no one answered. The upside down sleigh dumped Arthur, Bryony, Grandsanta, Dasher, and Gwen's bike out onto the dunes of a deserted beach before disappearing into the starry sky.

After a moment, Arthur stood up and walked across the sand, away from the others and Gwen's gift.

"Don't leave me, Arthur!" Grandsanta exclaimed.

But Arthur just kept walking.

"Poor old man and his reindeer, on our own at Christmas," Grandsanta said pitifully. When Arthur continued to walk away, the old man added, "At least have the decency to finish us off with a rock!"

The young man walked toward the vast ocean, his sadness as deep as the sea itself.

With no other way to keep warm in the predawn chill on the beach, Bryony tore small bits of wrapping paper off Gwen's bicycle to feed a campfire. The night had been such a wild rollercoaster of emotions:

shock at finding the undelivered gift, the excitement of embarking on the "impossible" mission, joy at finding Trelew, confusion on discovering it was the wrong Trelew, and now despair as even Arthur seemed resigned to failure. Worse than that, the young man had lost that most precious spark: his belief in the goodness of Santa Claus.

Arthur's sadness chilled the elf even more than the wild wind on that dark Cuban beach. Even his self-centered grandfather hated to see Arthur so low.

"Sun'll be up soon. It's Christmas!" Grandsanta reminded him.

Arthur's sour expression did not change at all. "Christmas is for kids. You grow out of it."

Bryony could not believe her pointed ears. "What, in the last six minutes?"

Arthur sighed. "You were right, Grandsanta. I wasn't normal."

The old man regretted his harsh words. "No, no, it's how you are, Son . . ."

Arthur interrupted. "No, you were right. And Steve. And . . . and Dad. All that trouble for one kid, I was being ridiculous."

He stretched out on the cold sand. Soon he would be able to sunbathe. Arthur wondered what that would be like. "This is nice. It's good to get away from it all, you know, all the Christmas fuss."

Grandsanta moved closer. "The night I last took Evie out, when there was all that . . . fuss . . . your father came to me. I'll never forget it. Couldn't look me in the eye. 'Dad,' he says, 'Steve thinks it's best you don't fly again. We're scrapping the sleigh.' Me own son. Who used to sit where you sat, looking up at me!"

The old man tried to explain his actions. "I just wanted them to remember who I used to be."

Grandsanta came as close as he could to apologizing. "We're just a fambly, Son. But we're a fambly of Santas! We're the Clauses!"

Arthur pulled Gwen's letter from his pocket. "Are we? How can I ever write another letter saying Santa cares?"

He threw the letter on the sand, pulled off his remaining reindeer slipper and tossed it far out to sea.

"G'night, Dad," he told the indifferent ocean. "Sleep well."

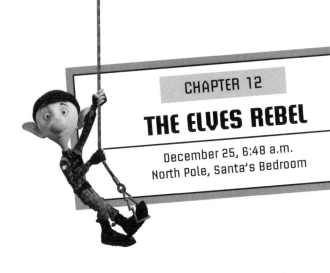

IN HIS NORTH Pole quarters, Santa slept quite soundly, snoring loudly beside Mrs. Claus in their big, cozy bed. A soft knock at the door roused the tired man from his slumbers.

Santa stumbled out of bed and opened the door to a hallway full of elves! An elf named Norah spoke for the group, "Sir, we know you shouldn't believe in rumors, but we do."

The Scottish elf called Seamus Malone stood beside her. He continued in his thick brogue, "Is it true you missed a child?"

"No, no," Santa hastily denied. But then, "Well . . . er . . . in a way . . . yes."

The gathered elves gasped.

"It was just one," Santa quickly added. "In fact,

not even that, zero point lots more zeroes, then a number with some sort of percent at the end. Not really an error! Just a . . . a one."

"One child doesn't matter? Which one?" asked an elf.

Santa squirmed. "Well I . . . um . . . it's not that . . ."

As more elves started murmuring about ones and children, Santa suggested, "Um . . . why don't you ask Steve? He can explain. Fiendishly clever . . ."

Keenly aware of the chain-of-command, Field Sergeant Andrew Marino asked, "But aren't you in charge, sir?"

"Of course . . . I'm Santa!" Santa asserted.

Thomas Jack still couldn't grasp Santa's loopy logic. "Sir, if the one that got missed doesn't matter, why have Arthur and Grandsanta gone to deliver the present?"

Santa's mouth dropped open. Behind him, in the open doorway, Mrs. Claus glared at her husband like a thundercloud about to spit lightning. "Malcolm, what's this about Arthur?!" she demanded fiercely.

In Mission Control, Steve soon found himself similarly surrounded by upset elves.

Deborah wanted to know, "Is there a list of children who don't matter?"

Carlos Connor misquoted, "Santa said they don't matter 100 percent."

"No, no, no," Steve quickly denied. "I . . . yes, of course." Steve stumbled, unable to collect his thoughts while so many tiny pairs of eyes stared at him accusingly.

Another elf asked, "Is it true children aren't even real?"

Steve sighed. "Look, I festivized every single country in the world! See? This one, this one, this one, this one, all of them! I mean, who cares about one single child?" he demanded defensively.

The elves gasped in horror at Steve's callous statement—especially because they saw who was standing right behind him. Santa and Mrs. Claus stared at the bank of screens, all showing sightings of Arthur and the old sleigh.

Santa exclaimed, "Arthur! The poor boy . . . Why on Earth would he . . . You're his brother, Steve. How could you let him . . . ?"

Even as he tried to push the blame on his elder son, Santa felt those tiny eyes boring into him. He quickly added, "And . . . um . . . about this child you missed. I'm really not sure you made the right decision."

Steve smiled coldly at his father. "Right. Over there is satellite tracking . . . navigation . . . data analysis . . . communications. Coffee machine's by the door. Goodnight, SANTA."

Then he walked out of the room singing, "Glooooooria, Hosannah in excelsis!"

Steve slammed the door behind him, leaving Santa alone with a thousand elves all looking at him for a solution. He stared around the room, feeling completely lost.

"Um . . . I'll be right back," he muttered.

He scuttled out the door. Santa did not know what to do. But his feet seemed to know where they wanted to go. They led him down the long Mailroom Department hall to the office of Mail Agent 3776.

Santa flicked on the light in Arthur's office, realizing he had never before bothered to visit. When he saw the shelf full of knickknacks, and the icon of Santa Claus, he felt both amazed and embarrassed by the young man's deep devotion to Christmas.

Santa slumped into the chair where his son had spent so many hours answering children's letters. He picked up a few and skimmed them. Santa immediately recognized Arthur's humor and goodwill in each sincere, sunny answer.

Dear Xiao-Ling, thanks for your letter and drawing of Santa tripping over your dog. It was hilarious . . .

Dear Alessandro, yes Santa is real. Tell your sister . . .

Dear Lars, I promise, Santa will come . . . He's the greatest man ever . . .

Santa looked up from the letters to the picture of the apple-cheeked, twinkly-eyed Saint on Arthur's wall. This magical, mystical Santa seemed so much more wonderful than the tired mortal Malcolm had been admiring in his mirror lately.

Santa no longer felt as if he filled the red suit—at least not where it really counted. His belly had grown bigger with the years, but had he somehow lost the heart of Santa Claus? Feeling more like ordinary old Malcolm, the current Claus wondered where his second son could be—and would he ever see Arthur again?

❄   ❄   ❄

At that moment, Bryony put the last bit of wrapping on the dying fire. She picked up Gwen's letter, but hesitated. "Can I burn this?"

Arthur shrugged. "Sure. There's millions like it."

He traced a skinny finger through the cold sand, idly drawing a picture of Santa. Then he wiped away the image as he mused, "This is how it feels to stop believing in Santa."

Arthur turned to the fire. "This is how Gwen will feel. Life is disappointing. People let you down."

Her large, childish handwriting tugged at his heart. "She's only six!"

He stared miserably at Gwen's crayon drawing

of burning Santa now starting to burn itself. Then Arthur suddenly snatched the singed letter and smoking postcard from the flames. He blew on them and exclaimed, "That's not Dad. Or you. Or Steve!"

He held up Gwen's childish scrawl depicting the jolly man in the red suit. "This is Santa! Gwen's Santa!" Arthur spoke with sudden conviction, "And as long as the bike is there when Gwen wakes up, then Santa came. And *he* cares!"

At the sound of heavy panting, the three travelers looked up. Dasher trotted to the campfire. His fur dripped with seawater. He dropped something soggy at Arthur's feet.

Arthur snatched up the sopping slipper. Then he grabbed the bike from Bryony and ran off along the shore. The relentless (and apparently water-resistant) slipper started to play its tune, and the young man sang jauntily along. "Jingle bells, jingle bells, jingle all the way . . ."

Concerned for Arthur's sanity, Bryony and Grandsanta followed, with Dasher on their heels. When he found a dinghy on the shore, Arthur pushed it into the surf. Then he scrawled a quick note in the sand: SORRY, I BORROWED THIS! Bryony and Grandsanta hurried into the boat to keep an eye on Arthur.

Arthur rowed with all his might, but he wasn't much of an oarsman, so he wound up splashing around in circles. Bryony had found her Hoho, and Steve's recorded voice droned over its speaker. "4,227 miles, then slight right . . ."

Grandsanta shook his head. "I've seen this before. 'Sleigh fever,' they call it: Pressure of Christmas drives a man loony. Santa Claus the Sixteenth got it, 1802. Every child that year got a sausage nailed to a piece of bark."

Bryony gently asked, "Arthur, do you really think you can row the whole Atlantic Ocean in the next . . ." She consulted her Hoho, ". . . thirty-seven minutes?"

"It's not too late yet. I just have to keep going."

Grandsanta looked around the small boat. "We need a blunt instrument. Knock him out and regroup."

Steve's recorded voice droned on, "Make a legal U-turn, then slight right in 4,228 miles."

Bryony tried to bring Arthur back to his senses. "You do know we're going around in circles?"

Grandsanta looked up, struck by a new idea. "You know, we're not the only ones. Maybe I *will* see Evie again . . ."

"What do you mean?" Arthur wondered.

Grandsanta explained, "Reindeer are brave, powerful beasts. But they're also silly fur-balls with twigs on their heads. They'll just keep going in a straight line right around the world! They'll be a thousand feet above us, flying at unimaginable speed, but they'll pass right over our heads!"

The three gazed up into the sky. Arthur spoke with wild excitement. "Then we CAN get the sleigh back!"

❋   ❋   ❋

Meanwhile, in Brussels, the high command of UNFITA (United Northern Federal International Treaty Alliance) gathered to discuss the ominous UFO. Chief Elinora De Silva tried to understand the babble of "intelligence" filling the busy war room.

"Maintaining course 760 . . . ," one operative observed.

"It's circling the globe!" a second added.

A third announced, "Ma'am, the UFO has gone into orbit!"

De Silva heard their words, but what did any of it mean?

❋   ❋   ❋

Similarly, Grandsanta understood Arthur's plan, but he still thought his grandson had lost his mind. "You?! Up there?! Catch that?! With this?!"

Arthur nodded, taking the boat's anchor from the old man's hands and adding two words, "Magic dust!"

Bryony pulled an Emergency Cracker from her kit.

"You crack it over your head," she explained. "You'll have to focus. The sleigh'll be coming at you at 45,000 miles an hour."

Arthur's breath came in desperate, shallow gasps. "Forty-five thousand . . ."

"You'll be torn in half!" Grandsanta worried.

"Depends on the angle the sleigh hits. You might just get beheaded," Bryony amended.

Arthur shuddered. "I've got a phobia of being beheaded! And heights and speed and reindeer and buttons . . ."

Bryony hadn't heard that one before. "Buttons?"

"I'm pretty much scared of everything!" Arthur admitted.

Then he muttered miserably to himself, "Gwen thinks you're coming . . . Oh, no, I can't do it . . . yes, you can . . . no, you can't . . . Yes, I can . . . come on, Arthur!"

Grandsanta tried to comfort him. "Don't worry, son. Only a raving lunatic would . . ."

"I have to worry! It's the only thing I'm good at!" Arthur exclaimed, adding with a sudden inspiration. "Worry me!"

"The sleigh'll be back any minute," Bryony observed.

"C'mon! Worry me quickly!" Arthur urged.

Grandsanta looked at him with growing understanding of Arthur's odd request. "Imagine Gwen! All alone, nothing under the tree!"

Arthur nodded. "Here we go!"

He pulled the cracker! In a flash, Bryony tied a roll of ribbon around his waist, and Arthur floated up like a balloon on a string, shaking wildly!

His fear of heights kicked in, and he gasped, "Aaaahhh! No, I don't like this! Stop! Stop! Stop! Get me DOWN!"

Grandsanta went on, "Imagine the tears as she finds she's been left out!"

Bryony realized what the old man was doing, so she added, ". . . screaming, 'SANTA DIDN'T COME!'"

Arthur's focus returned, but only briefly. "Oh, Gwen . . . No, no! I'm just too high!"

Grandsanta and Bryony urged him on, their shouts receding as he floated higher, and the wind filled his big ears.

". . . Gwen in the street, surrounded by kids on new bikes, pointing, 'That's the girl that Santa HATES!' She runs away, drops out of school . . ."

Grandsanta jumped in, "Her childish heart broken, she may never build a snowman again!"

Arthur looked down and his head spun with dizziness and a new fear. "Aaaagh! But what if there are buttons on the sleigh I don't know about?!"

The moment of truth had arrived, Bryony screamed, "Here it IS!"

Still upside down and traveling faster than a speeding bullet, the sleigh approached almost before Arthur's eyes could perceive it. He swung the anchor, but before he could throw it, the metal hook snagged the reindeer harness and whipped Arthur into the sleigh's wake.

SNAP! The ribbon broke as the sleigh shot away with Arthur trailing after it, helpless as a tin can tied behind a car of newlyweds.

But Arthur wasn't a tin can. He was a young man, terrified out of his wits, but determined to achieve his goal. He somehow gathered the strength to pull himself along that wildly-whipping rope, toward the sleigh soaring above the sea.

In the boat far below, Bryony and Grandsanta tried not to worry. Finally, Bryony broke the nervous silence. "How do you think he's . . . um . . ."

"Fine. Fine," Grandsanta said hastily. "Probably just . . ."

The whole sleigh flipped over. Shaking and screaming, Arthur was bounced from the back of the sleigh all the way to the front. He grabbed onto the nearest reindeer's antlers. He soon found himself nose to nose with the beast. But the reindeer was upside down and still running!

He pulled himself farther, up to the belly of the beast, only to be surrounded by flailing hooves. Arthur held onto the fragile harness, hoping against hope that it would not break.

In the boat below, Bryony and Grandsanta continued their awkward vigil. "So, um . . . how come they didn't scrap the sleigh, sir?" Bryony wondered.

"I threatened the elves," Grandsanta explained. "Said I'd feed 'em to the polar bears."

Bryony didn't know what to say to that. So she fished a treat out of her pocket and offered it to the old man. "Um . . . fig roll, sir?"

Arthur managed to climb toward the center of the jingling harness. Unfortunately, the harness broke and released yet another reindeer. Arthur dangled from one arm, swinging almost as uncontrollably as the metal deer logo.

Bryony and Grandsanta had nothing to do now except worry. As the silence grew from merely uncomfortable to downright miserable, Grandsanta nervously sighed. "Elf, how do you fancy being the one to tell his parents about all this?"

CHAPTER 13

EVERYBODY PANIC!

December 25, 7:05 a.m.
Atlantic Ocean
Distance to Trelew: 4,227 miles

ARTHUR COULD NOT imagine telling anyone about this amazing adventure. Who would believe him? Arthur himself could not believe he was this high up, traveling this fast, and clambering over big beasts to try to reach an upside down sleigh. Yet he was!

Astride a flying reindeer, the young man afraid of, well, everything, somehow found the courage to leap from the beast's back to the sleigh! Arthur grabbed the reins, and then lunged for the handbrake.

WHOOSH! Once again, the sleigh dropped like a stone!

Bryony and Grandsanta heard a whistle and a jingling. They looked up just in time to see the sleigh speeding right for them!

The impact of the reindeer smashing into the small

boat sent Grandsanta, Bryony, and Dasher bouncing into the air. Then the sleigh splashed down into the sea, and the three landed inside it—with Dasher's warm, furry rear end pressed into Arthur's face.

Normally, such close proximity to his grandfather's pet would have frightened Arthur. But instead, he laughed!

Bryony cheered. "Yay, Arthur! You did it! You did it!"

Arthur marveled, "I . . . I did it with worry!"

Bryony hugged him. "Oh, I was sure you'd die! It was great!"

Steve's voice interrupted this emotional moment, as Bryony's Hoho3000 slowly sank, along with the wrecked boat. Its navigation program commanded robotically, "Proceed to the highlighted route. Procee . . . *gurgle, glub.*"

Grandsanta wasn't concerned about the loss of the GPS. He said, "Just keep worrying about Gwen. I'll find a way there, boy. Whatever it takes." He cracked the reins and cried, "To Trelew!" With a *WHOOSH* and a splash, the sleigh took off.

At the North Pole, Santa Claus had reached a decision. He burst into his bedroom and told his wife, "Margaret! Hand me my Me suit! All sorted! Steve's . . . um . . . holding the fort, while

I . . . er . . . deliver the present. Yes! And find Arthur and Father!"

The ever-supportive Mrs. Claus said, "Well done, dear."

But she was already dressed and closing her coat. Mrs. Claus continued, "Trelew's on a course of 187.7 degrees from the geographic pole, but as it's the old sleigh, we should allow a drift margin of 1,000 miles either side of the Greenwich meridian."

She paused to show Santa what she had packed for their journey. "I've got a sweater for Arthur, your father's pills, and some nice, sweet tea."

Santa put on his red jacket, eager to get the mission over with—and glad for his wife's capable company.

Despite Santa's reassurance that their older son was "holding the fort," Steve had no idea the S-1 was leaving the dock. So Steve was completely shocked when his room suddenly started to shake. Only one force in the whole North Pole complex had the power to shake its icy foundations—his beloved ship!

BANG!

Steve winced at a second loud noise, even more ominous than the first. What was going on? Who would be crazy enough to try to steal the S-1?!

Steve ran down what felt like an endless hall toward the dock doors. He carried his Santa suit. His doting assistant chased after him, wondering what was wrong. "Sir? SIR!" Peter cried.

Steve did not answer. He was too busy reading the sticky note stuck to the dock door:

Popped out to take present.

Turkey sandwich in the fridge.

Mum and Dad

Steve fumed, blaming his brother for the disaster. "That idiot, Arthur!" He opened the dock door and scrambled under. To his horror, Steve saw the S-1 heaving forward, straining at the steel cables holding it to its moorings.

The ship slammed against an ice wall, denting its shiny hull. Steve's fists clenched. Arthur had really made a mess this time! This was even worse than flooding the elf barracks. This was an outrage of epic proportions; enough to get the fool banished from the North Pole—if Steve had anything to say about it.

Steve ranted, "He's driven everyone crazy! He'll destroy Christmas!"

Peter added the very worst thing he could imagine, "And you'll never get to be Santa!"

Steve glanced back at the loyal-but-boneheaded elf. Then he dashed forward and closed the door behind him, locking Peter out.

"Steeeevennn!" Peter protested.

The chaos aboard the S-1 was even more maddening than that on the dock. Alarms blared. Screens flashed. Doors swished open and closed, and the special red Santa carpet rolled and unrolled rapidly as Santa pushed random buttons trying to get the complicated ship off the ground.

With two clumsy, chubby fingers, Santa pecked Gwen's address into the ship's navigation system. "Um . . . 23 Mimosa Avenue . . . Trelew."

The S-1 smashed into a wall. Everything shuddered! Mrs. Claus picked up a huge manual and scolded, "Really, Malcolm, there's no harm in using a manual." Then she muttered, "Men."

Santa felt sweat suddenly dampen the armpits of his red suit. He barked, "Margaret, I order you to disembark! It's not safe!"

He pressed a button and a coffee machine popped up.

Mrs. Claus made no move to obey her husband's command. "Piffle. I did a microlight flying course on the Internet. It can't be that different."

But it was! She started pressing buttons. A door opened and the couple spun around to discover Steve glaring at them.

Santa felt as helpless as a rat in a trap. "Steve!"

His son wasted no time accusing, "You've dented it! You take it out without asking and . . ."

Mrs. Claus jumped in. "Malcolm, you told me he knew! You know how Steve feels about his S-1."

Santa struggled to defend himself. "It's my S-1! S for *Santa*. *I'm* flying to this child . . ."

"Of course, she's all that matters," Steve replied. "Not me, your son. Not the two billion things I did right tonight, nooo!"

Santa sighed. "This is about the pool table I never gave you, isn't it? I told you, you should've written to me."

Steve hated being treated like just another child. "I was eight! You're my DAD!"

Mrs. Claus raised her voice, "FOR GOODNESS SAKE! Arthur and Grandsanta are out there, probably not wearing nearly enough layers, and you two are bickering over a big red toy?"

Santa tried to regain control. "If Steven could just stand back and . . ."

An airbag exploded into Santa and oxygen masks dropped. Santa's shoulders slumped in defeat. "You drive, Steven."

Steve nodded, "Thank you." Then he put on his red leather driving gloves and took the helm. Steve went on, "So, since gift delivery to Child 47785BXK is all that seems to matter, I'll do it myself. Then we'll pick up Arthur and Grandsanta from whatever ditch they ended up in."

He switched the S-1 into Premium Velocity.

In seconds, the high-tech craft rocketed down an ice tunnel, gathering speed with every yard.

Steve wasn't the only one awakened by the S-1's roaring engine. Support elves swarmed Mission Control to stare at screens showing the ship's sudden departure.

Helmsman Tankenson jumped to a grim conclusion. "They're deserting us!"

The Scottish elf beside him agreed, "The Santas are leaving!"

An older Scottish elf moaned in his thick brogue. "It's like 1816! Elves, into hiding with you!"

"Abandon the North Pole!" another elf shouted over the general panic.

"No, stop!" Peter yelled over the crowed, but no one listened.

An elf ran to one of the control panels and lifted up a little flap with a red button underneath. Its label read, DELETE CHRISTMAS. The elf paused, then pressed the button. Immediately alarms started sounding. Flashing lights added to the chaos. Computer screens began shutting down, as if a terrible virus had infected the system.

Suddenly, a robotic voice sounded, "North Pole Meltdown in 10 minutes."

"Everybody panic!" an elf yelled.

Peter stood in the middle of a crowd, horrified. "It's Arthur! He's destroying Christmas! And Steven will never come back!" he yelled. But no one was listening. They were too busy running for the exits.

CHAPTER 14

THE BIGGEST MAP IN THE WORLD

December 25, 7:15 a.m.
Atlantic Ocean
Time until Sunrise: 34 minutes

EVEN AS PETER spoke, the sleigh rose higher than any sleigh has ever gone before. Beyond fear, Arthur held Eve's side giddily.

Grandsanta exclaimed, "I know where we can find a map, lad!"

As the sleigh kept climbing straight up into the stratosphere Grandsanta hit a button and old World War II gas masks popped up. Eve shook and the reindeer snorted with the effort.

"A bit risky this. Never tried it before," Grandsanta admitted as the sleigh rose even higher, and suddenly the reindeer started to float!

The sleigh soared into space, past a huge satellite hanging silently in the black void. As the shivering, weightless passengers hung on for dear life, Grandsanta pointed in triumph. "There! THE BIGGEST MAP IN THE WORLD!"

Arthur followed the old man's finger. What did his grandfather mean? Then he suddenly recognized the round, marbled object below them: *It was Earth!*

The blue masses were oceans; the white swirls, clouds; and that greenish, brown patch was Europe. He could see England. They would find Trelew!

Grandsanta, Bryony, and Arthur cheered. Then a bright flash glinted over the rim of the globe. Dawn crept west, toward England!

Grandsanta flicked the reins, and the sleigh dashed back down toward their destination. As Eve touched the exosphere, her runners turned red hot. Would the sleigh burn before they could reach Cornwall? Arthur remembered the crayon drawing of the burning Santa Claus on Gwen's postcard. Was it about to come true?

Unknown to the young man, there also lurked another danger. The craft's fiery progress excited the military leaders gathered at UNFITA's headquarters.

Chief De Silva addressed them gravely. "Friends, on this night of peace we stand confronted by an unknown enemy."

Her aide interrupted, handing her a phone. "Ma'am. The British Prime Minister."

De Silva spoke into the receiver. "Prime Minister? Chief De Silva."

A surprisingly shrill voice replied. "Um, hello? Shoot down the red thing!"

The Chief felt confused. Had she heard the high voice correctly? She asked, "I'm sorry?"

"It's not a sleigh . . . it's aliens! Bad aliens! From space!" the shrill voice shrieked over the speakerphone.

The assembled generals reacted to this strange assertion. "Aliens!" "Bad aliens?" "Thought so . . ." "Oh dear!" If they thought the voice sounded too high and even childish to belong to the Prime Minister, no one dared mention this.

The shrill rant continued. "They're heading for England! Tell the British army to shoot 'em down!"

Chief De Silva did not recognize the voice. "Who did you say this was?"

In the North Pole's Mission Control, Peter panicked. His plan had seemed so perfect. But now he feared his fib would fail. So he quickly concluded, "I'm the British king . . . I mean Prime Minister! I'm not an elf!"

Then he slammed down the phone and drank another espresso.

When the odd voice gave way to a dial tone, De Silva hung up, too. Then she addressed the generals.

"Even if that wasn't the British Prime Minister, we must take this seriously."

"But . . . what if the aliens come in peace?" the French general wondered.

The Canadian general reminded them, "It terrorized Toronto. I say we shoot it from the sky. Shoot down the red thing!"

Other generals agreed. "Shoot it down!" "Come on! "Shoot down the red thing!"

✳   ✳   ✳

As Eve entered the atmosphere, gravity made her go even faster! "Hold tight, lad, this is where it gets really rough," Grandsanta warned.

The sleigh shuddered. Rivets and panels rattled. The harness smoked and singed in the heat. *SNAP!* A rein broke, and another reindeer left the team.

Grandsanta struggled to control the speeding sleigh. He handed one of the reins to Arthur, pleading, "Help me out, lad!"

Together, the two Clauses managed to hold the sleigh on course, even as sparks shot out of Eve's joints and the magic dust tank rattled ominously.

BOOM! A small explosion rocked the speeding sleigh and two reindeer were blasted free in clouds of sparking dust.

Arthur and Grandsanta looked at the harness.

Only one "deer" remained—the hollow metal logo swiped from the roof of the tractor dealership. The sleigh nose-dived, and the logo started to melt!

Grandsanta felt a familiar hoof climbing over him. "Not now, you sack of antlers!" he groused at his pet.

But Dasher wasn't trying to cuddle in his master's lap. The loyal reindeer was determined to pull that sleigh!

Dasher climbed over Grandsanta to the front of the sleigh. He jumped into the stream of sparkling magic dust. Dasher grabbed the harness in his teeth and kicked the molten logo away.

Their hope rekindled, the passengers cheered. "Woohoo!" Grandsanta whooped.

❄   ❄   ❄

In the UNFITA war room, claxons blared, and the speaker system reported, "Alert Level 6. Shoot Down Red Thing. Shoot Down Red Thing."

De Silva's aide announced, "Red thing reentering troposphere, ma'am."

An operative staring at a screen added, "On radar in 40 seconds."

Another counted down, "Visual in 46 . . . 45 . . ."

❄   ❄   ❄

With each passing second, the globe grew closer to the hurtling sleigh. Bryony worried, "They'll be watching, sir. They tracked us all around the world. Any minute now they'll have us in their sights."

"They think we're aliens!" Arthur exclaimed.

"All their technology against my Evie," Grandsanta fretted.

"Are you afraid, sir?" the elf asked.

"Never been afraid of anything in me life!" Grandsanta declared. "Except looking like an old fool."

Arthur shrugged. "I always look like a fool. It's the only thing I'm not scared of."

Grandsanta met his grandson's gaze, and they shared a smile. The old man winked. "Let's give 'em something to shoot at!"

Then he flipped a little lid over a button with one mysterious word printed on it: *WAR*. As soon as he pressed the button, camouflage panels started clanking into place. But these did not make Eve look like a steam train.

The UNFITA operative concluded his countdown and stated, "We have visual!"

Chief De Silva, the generals, and UNFITA operatives stared at the screen in disbelief.

How on earth could a World War I German Fokker Triplane be speeding toward England? Surely the Red Baron had not returned to attack!

As the "plane" flew over the famous White Cliffs

of Dover, Arthur peeped over the edge. "England! We're nearly there!" he told his companions.

Bryony looked thoughtful. "It's quiet!"

Grandsanta seemed worried. "Too quiet."

"Maybe they all went to bed so they wouldn't be too tired for Christmas!" Arthur suggested.

But his optimistic assertion proved quite wrong. With the "Red Baron" in their sights, the UNFITA operatives reported, "I have the Red Thing. Coordinate G567. Altitude 11,000 feet. Red Thing coming to me."

De Silva commanded, "Target its controls. Electronics, navigation, propulsion systems."

Her aide scanned the sleigh, "Ma'am, it doesn't have any. The engine appears to be . . . furry."

Inside the antique camouflage, Dasher's sides heaved and the old deer panted. Even in his youth, such a fast flight would have been challenging. But the ancient, one-antlered pet had not trained for this mission. Dasher had spent decades doing little more than dozing at Grandsanta's feet.

Arthur, Bryony, and Grandsanta glanced back in concern at the growing glint of sunlight on the horizon behind them. The sleigh struggled like a plane with a sputtering engine.

Grandsanta cranked up the "hooves per second."

Then all three shouted encouragement to the tired reindeer. "Come on, lad!" "You can do it!" "Put your back into it!"

Arthur pressed his reindeer slipper to start "Jingle Bells." Then he began singing and the others joined in!

"Dashing through the snow, in a one horse open sleigh . . ."

The song lifted Dasher's spirits, giving his legs new strength.

"Over the field we go, laughing all the way . . ."

Bryony's silvery elfin laugh echoed, "Ha, ha, ha . . ."

BLEEP! BLEEP! BLEEP! BLEEP! The sensors sounded in UNFITA's war room. An operative reported, "I am picking up an electronic signal on the sensors! It's very faint, but . . ."

"Scramble weapons," De Silva commanded. So the mysterious craft had an electromagnetic frequency after all!

The "triplane" flew over snow-covered countryside with the sunlight close behind. The sun seemed in danger of catching the sleigh at any moment. Unwilling to let that happen, Dasher galloped with all his might, encouraged by his passengers, who sang along with the slipper, "Jingle Bells, Jingle Bells, Jingle all the way!"

CHAPTER 15

ATTACK!

December 25, 7:35 a.m.
Location: TRELEW!
Time until Sunrise: 14 minutes

ARTHUR STUDIED GWEN'S postcard with its jaunty tourist map of Cornwall. He recognized the village of Trelew dead ahead! Arthur exclaimed, "That's it there! We made it!"

Then something sped toward them. At first just a tiny speck, it suddenly became clearer: A UNFITA drone, laden with deadly missiles!

Grandsanta saw the drone and replied grimly. "Not quite. We haven't made it yet."

The old man swerved the sleigh, but this proved futile against such advanced technology.

"Drone closing . . . ," the UNFITA operative told his boss.

"It's locked onto us," Bryony observed. "It's tracking something electronic!"

Grandsanta puzzled, "We haven't got any electrickery! Just wood and brass and . . ."

The tinny sound of "Jingle Bells" rose from the floor. They shouted to Arthur, "Your SLIPPER!"

The operative concluded, "We have a lock!"

In the speeding sleigh, Grandsanta grabbed the singing slipper. "Give it here. I'll create a diversion!"

"But you're coming, too!" Bryony exclaimed. "You'll land the sleigh on the roof with the reindeer and the jingly bells and . . . tell him Arthur!"

Grandsanta shook his gray head. "You were right, Arthur. It doesn't matter how Santa's gift gets there. It doesn't even matter if it's Mr. Postman in his spaceship. As long as it gets there."

"But you and Evie?" Arthur's eyes filled with tears.

Grandsanta laughed gallantly. "Ha! I'll be fine! Now, do as I say . . ."

In the war room, the operative's voice grew tense as he began the countdown to detonation. "In range in 3 seconds . . . 2 seconds . . ."

The "Red Baron" filled the giant screen as the drone closed in on its target. Then suddenly the triplane exploded! Bits of camouflage hurtled toward the screen, a confusing array, including not only the antique plane, but a house, a steam train, a ship, and then . . . *SPLAT!*

The drone's camera was suddenly hit with sticky tangerines, then chocolate coins, candy canes, and a squishy little toy that waddled down the glass.

De Silva's aide exclaimed, "They're firing on us, ma'am! Chocolate coins and candy canes . . ."

Chief De Silva wondered, "Have you been into the eggnog?"

The bizarre barrage came from Bryony's stocking stuffer gun, which she fired at the drone from the sleigh's rear. When the gun ran out of its delicious and delightful ammunition, the elf turned to Grandsanta. The old man shouted to Arthur, "GO! Don't stop until you see the whites of her eyes!"

As Arthur jumped from under the sleigh, he pulled a cord. Something huge and scarlet opened above his head—the red velvet toy sack Grandsanta had once used to carry toys for all the children in the world.

As he drifted down toward England under his unique parachute, Arthur shouted, "Happy Christmas!"

Grandsanta addressed Bryony. "Go on, elf. You, too."

Bryony hesitated, wondering what would happen to the grouchy old man who had somehow become quite dear to her.

He quickly added, "I'll be fine."

But would he? Bryony could not be sure, any more than she could disobey a Claus. The elf's tiny eyes sparkled with tears as she kissed Grandsanta's grizzled cheek. Then she jumped!

Just then, Chief De Silva gave the fateful command, "Launch Missiles!"

In seconds, the drone fired. Grandsanta set the telltale slipper on Eve's dashboard and loosened Dasher's reins. He said, "This is it, old fella. Maybe the next Santa never sat in my Evie, but Arthur did, and he's as good a man as any Santa there's ever been."

As Dasher floated free, Grandsanta stood proudly atop his sleigh and saluted the loyal deer. Rockets zoomed closer, but the old man showed no fear. He simply said, "Bye, Evie!"

BOOM! The sleigh exploded brilliantly in the dark sky!

"Red thing down," the UNFITA operative reported.

De Silva concluded, "Thank you, gentlemen."

Meanwhile, in the sky above Trelew, Arthur and Bryony heard an alarming *RRRIPPP* in the fabric above them as ancient stitches tore free of the faded velvet. No longer gently floating, the two suddenly found themselves plummeting toward trees that grew larger every second!

*   *   *

At the same time, the S-1 swooped over Trelew. Steve prepared to exit the high-tech ship's camouflaged hatch in a slick, Armani-style suit, complete with silk tie. He looked more like a businessman than a figure of legend.

With an athlete's grace, and the wind ruffling his perfectly-coiffed hair, Steve rappelled down toward the address Santa had programmed into the S-1's sophisticated navigation system.

On his muscular back, Steve carried an unwrapped bicycle significantly more expensive than the one Gwen requested. He felt sure his delivery would be met with great delight.

As his parents watched Steve on the S-1's screen, both fretted about the fate of their other son.

Santa sighed. "Poor Arthur. He tried so hard . . . but he's flunked again."

Mrs. Claus tried to comfort him. "Of course he hasn't, dear! We're here. The little girl will get her present. I think he's done rather splendidly."

On Mimosa Avenue, Steve pressed a bell and a child quickly opened the door. Steve immediately launched into his speech, "Good morning, Gwen. Ho, ho, etcetera. Apologies for the minor delay, but I'm sure even a child can understand that in an operation as complex as Christmas there's always an insignificant margin of error, which is you."

Barely taking a breath, he went on, "As a gesture, I've upgraded you to the Glamorfast Ultra X-3, which retails at substantially more than your requested gift. Bigger, ergo, better," Steve concluded as he wheeled the bike toward the child. Then he held out a paper and pen, "You wouldn't mind just signing a legal waiver?"

Pedro stared at Steve. He had not understood one word of the strange man's speech. But the boy sure liked the bike!

He spoke in rapid Spanish, *"No le entiendo, señor. Soy Pedro."*

Steve stared back at the boy and echoed, "Pedro? A boy?"

"Quién es usted?" Pedro asked the stranger in the odd red suit. His small hands tightened their grip on the shiny bike.

Steve struggled to understand this unthinkable situation. "A Spanish boy? This is an error. *No hablo español.* Get off the bike!" Steve had gone to the wrong Trelew as well!

Steve grabbed for the Glamorfast Ultra X-3, but Pedro clung to it and then burst into tears! His small, slipper-loving dog ran out the door and latched onto Steve's foot.

"No, no, no!" Steve exclaimed. "Please don't cry. *NO CRYO!*"

The stranger's loud voice frightened the boy. So Pedro wailed louder. "PAPAAAAAAA!!!"

Steve pleaded, *"No sob-idad!"*

❄ ❄ ❄

As Steve struggled to comprehend how his simple mission could have gone so wrong, Arthur and Bryony staggered out of the woods near the English Trelew. Arthur had bumped his leg against a tree trunk upon landing and was limping.

Worse than the pain was the realization that dawn approached faster than they could possibly reach the village below. Bryony whined with frustration, "It's over a mile. We've got no sleigh, no reindeer, and you can't even walk properly!"

Arthur blinked, unwilling to accept defeat after all that they'd been through. He found inspiration.

Arthur ripped the paper off Gwen's small bike. Horrified to see the gorgeous wrapping destroyed, Bryony demanded, "What are you doing?"

Arthur pulled down the training wheels and leaped on the little bicycle. "I can cycle!" And before the elf could say another word, Arthur took off down the hill.

Bryony ran after him, crying, "Come back! What about the wrapping?"

As the little bike rolled swiftly toward Trelew, Arthur consulted Gwen's postcard. "The church! She lives by the church."

Though his leg hurt, and his knees kept knocking into the handlebars, Arthur's heart felt light with renewed hope. As he sped past a pasture full of cows, the youngest Claus called out, "Happy Christmas, cows!"

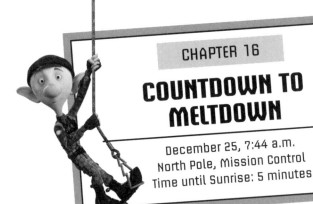

CHAPTER 16

COUNTDOWN TO MELTDOWN

December 25, 7:44 a.m.
North Pole, Mission Control
Time until Sunrise: 5 minutes

MEANWHILE AT THE North Pole, Mission Control suffered a literal meltdown. Disintegrating ice walls dripped down over hysterical elves abandoning their Claus-less headquarters.

Peter encouraged the crazed elves to destroy Santa's ice statue.

Then as suddenly as dawn defeats even the blackest night, a dot appeared on the screen showing Gwen's house. Ernie Clicker, Grandsanta's former Communications Chief spotted the dot and cried, "Hold on a minute. Look! It's Arthur. He's delivering the present!"

Carlos Connor seized on this good news. "No child left behind!"

Other elves stared at the screen, then cheered!

More elves rushed in to watch the amazing spectacle of the gawky young man pedaling through Trelew on a small, pink bicycle with an elf chasing after him.

"You're getting it dirty!" Bryony scolded as the bike rolled past an alley.

Down the alley, Dasher sniffed at a trash bin, or as they say in England, a wheely bin. The deer peered inside and saw his beloved master slumped on the garbage like one more piece of trash. Confused, concussed, and covered in filth, Grandsanta was nevertheless alive!

"Hello, young reindeer!" he said with groggy good cheer. "Which Christmas is this then?"

❄   ❄   ❄

Meanwhile, aboard the S-1, good cheer was in short supply. Steve stumbled up the mangled remains of the slick ship's red carpet and admitted, "OK, so I'm not great with children! Does that make me a bad Santa?"

When his father raised one white eyebrow at this dumb question, Steve turned on him. "You're hardly perfect. Let me guess, you put in the address, saw a list of Mimosa Avenues and just clicked on the first one? You're just like Arthur!"

"Am I?" Santa wondered. He was beginning to hope so.

Then the S-1 received a message from North Pole Mission Control. On the screen, Seamus Malone exclaimed, "Sir! The soldiers shot the sleigh!"

Mrs. Claus, Santa, and Steve gasped. What about Arthur and Grandsanta? Had they been shot down with the sleigh? Before the Claus's thoughts could grow too grim, Deborah added, "But sir, it's Arthur . . . He's still going!"

She and Seamus stepped back to reveal the cheering elves surrounding them shouting, "Arthur! Arthur!"

Steve blinked hard. What was his crazy brother doing now? Santa and Mrs. Claus felt relieved and amazed!

✳   ✳   ✳

WHIZZ! The pink Twinkle Bike came around a corner with its gangly rider pedaling madly, his bony knees poking up with each stroke. Breathless Bryony ran after him, shouting, "No one gets an unwrapped present on my watch!"

Even as she ran, the determined little elf started wrapping the rolling bike. "Stand up!" she told Arthur. When he obeyed, she wrapped the seat.

"Finger!" she commanded, and Arthur put his finger on the wrapping paper while Bryony expertly secured it with tape.

Arthur exclaimed, "The church!"

Bryony slid to the side of the bike and called, "Right foot!"

When Arthur lifted up his foot, she wrapped the pedal.

"Left foot!" the elf continued as the bike neared its destination.

"Hands up!" Bryony barked like a cop stopping a criminal.

Arthur obediently lifted both hands so the elf could climb up and wrap the handlebars. Then he suddenly realized they were heading straight for a wall! "Ahhhh!"

Arthur grabbed a signpost and swung the bike around. The bike smashed into a snowman! When Bryony looked up, they were still zooming down the street, but now Arthur wore the snowman's hat and pipe.

The Mission Control elves cheered! "In Santa We Believe!" they shouted. "Arthur! Arthur!"

"Nearly there!" Arthur cried as he popped up the front wheel. But the sunlight was nearly there, too! Bryony scrambled to wrap the front wheel as she could barely wrap and hang on.

The bike rounded the corner, and they started down Mimosa Avenue. Arthur spotted number 23. "That's it there!"

"Back wheel—ready?" Bryony asked as she tucked up the training wheels.

Arthur wobbled, but he did not fall. "Whooaaaa . . ."

"Here we go!" Bryony thrust a wrapping paper tube between the spokes, and the bike flipped up and over the mailbox from which Gwen mailed her letter to Santa.

The bike soared into the air, flying over a squirrel in a tree.

Arthur let go of the bike in mid-air and landed in a snowdrift. The perfectly wrapped bike dropped into his lap! He looked for Bryony, but the elf was caught in the tree lights. "Elf down!" she exclaimed, prepared to let Arthur continue without her. "Go on. Quick!" she urged.

But Arthur hesitated. Instead, he leaned over and grabbed her ribbon, explaining, "There's always time for a bow."

CHAPTER 17

THREE SANTAS ON THE SCENE

December 25, 7:49 a.m.
23 Mimosa Avenue
Trelew, Cornwall, England
Time until Sunrise: NOW!

BUT WAS THERE time for a bow? Arthur looked up just as the red light of dawn crept across Gwen's house and glinted off her bedroom window!

The first ray of Christmas day fell on Gwen's face. She opened her eyes.

Arthur stared up in agony. "No! We can't be too late!"

Then something amazing happened: A huge shadow fell over Gwen's house, as if night itself were falling back down! Gwen shut her eyes and drifted dreamily back to sleep, completely unaware of the huge spaceship that had caused this curious eclipse.

As sunlight formed a halo around the S-1, Arthur climbed awkwardly through a window with Gwen's bike. Steve rappelled gracefully from the S-1, while his bulky father tumbled down clumsily.

And yet one more Santa approached Gwen's home. "Ho, ho, ho! Merry Christmas!" Grandsanta exclaimed as he rode down Mimosa Avenue.

The old man imagined himself riding in his beloved Evie, behind a team of gorgeous reindeer, wearing his beautiful red suit, and tossing candy and toys from his velvet sack. In truth, his "sleigh" was really a trash bin. His "team," a single, exhausted, one-antlered, ancient reindeer harnessed by "reins" made from Grandsanta's old clothes. His "suit" consisted only of his underwear. The "treats" he tossed were trash from a garbage bag. Yet in his delightful delusion, Grandsanta beamed a benevolent smile that was pure Santa Claus.

This spirit was not lost on the Mission Control elves. Their tiny eyes misted with tears as they watched the three Clauses converging on Gwen's house. Some sobbed, while others sang "White Christmas" and waved candles overhead.

Chris Tankenson remarked, "All the Santas are taking the missing present!"

Carlos Connor echoed, "It's beautiful!"

Norah agreed, "The whole family, spreading peace and goodwill!"

Ernie's voice choked with sweet emotion. "Gaw bless the Clauses!"

Steve used one of his high-tech devices to open the door. Santa squeezed through the bathroom window, while Grandsanta crashed down the chimney. Soot covered his wrinkled face and turned his underwear black, but his jolly mood remained unchanged.

Arthur crept toward Gwen's bed, moved by the aura of trust and innocence surrounding the sleeping child. He slipped a tag into her stocking that said, "Under the tree."

When he reached the hall, Arthur heard a noise. He looked downstairs and saw his father! The young man's face twitched with intense emotion.

Arthur raced to embrace Santa Claus. He gushed, "Dad?! You came! I knew you would! You wouldn't just go back to bed and forget Gwen! You're Santa!"

Knowing the sad truth, Santa felt ashamed. Especially when he saw in his son all that Santa should be.

But before he could say anything . . . *SMACK!* Steve bumped into them from one side and *THUMP!* Grandsanta from the other!

Steve grabbed the bike from Arthur. Grandsanta snatched it from Steve! To Arthur's dismay, a whispered tussle ensued; the pointless struggle reminded him of the ugly incident that had ruined Christmas earlier: the board game fiasco.

"I'm Santa! I'm delivering it!" Steve insisted.

"Don't be silly, I'm Santa, can't you see from my suit?" Grandsanta gestured toward his sooty underwear.

Santa jumped in, "I am actually Santa, and I think it would be best if I . . ."

Steve interrupted, "I'm Santa! You handed it over!"

"I didn't . . . in fact . . . technically . . ." Santa went on.

"You said I could drive," Steve pointed out.

"I'm Santa, you naughty boys!" Grandsanta scolded. Then he reached in his garbage bag. "Here, have a bonbon."

But Steve would not exchange the bike for a brown apple core, and neither would Santa. Finally Arthur hissed, "Shhhh!"

He pointed upstairs where a door creaked open. The three Clauses heard Gwen's high-pitched six-year-old voice exclaim, "It's Christmas!"

Arthur begged, "Please. Gwen just has to have a present from Santa!"

Santa looked at him gently, then said, "You do it, Arthur."

As she ran to her parents' room, Gwen's little feet padded overhead. "Mummy, Daddy, wake up!" she squeaked.

Arthur raced into the living room and carefully placed the present under the tree. At last, after so much effort, everything was set!

Then Grandsanta toddled in and merrily emptied his garbage bag under the tree, too! "Ho, ho, ho!" he chuckled, just as Gwen started down the stairs.

Santa and Steve dragged the old man toward a closet, as Arthur frantically scooped up all the trash.

"Father, please keep it down," Santa whispered urgently.

But the old man's joy would not be muted. "Merry Christmas, everyone!" he shouted behind the closed door.

Santa started to climb out the window. But Arthur tugged his red suit and whispered, "Dad! Wait. Please, let's . . ."

He nodded toward the living room. Arthur wanted to watch, to enjoy this sweet reward after the miserable night of seemingly endless struggle.

Santa looked surprised. "In all my years . . . I've never actually . . . always so busy."

Arthur eased the closet door open just a crack. Three generations of Santas bunched up to peer out.

Squashed between his sons, Santa looked from one to the other, his blue eyes moist with emotion. ". . . Too busy," he muttered. "I'm not good at . . . In my day, a pat on the back and a walnut went a long way . . ."

Both Arthur and Steve realized this was Santa's way of telling them that he loved them, and that he was sorry for all the years he'd been more of a red-and-white blur than a father. Gwen shouted impatiently, "Mummy, Daddy, come ON! Look! I got a note from Santa in my stocking. It says my present's under the tree!"

Light footsteps pattered downstairs. Gwen squealed with delight as she saw the big, brightly wrapped package under the twinkling tree.

"Oh look! What is it?" Gwen exclaimed as her small hands tore through the paper. "I'm almost through . . ."

The three Santas shivered with joy when they saw the look on the little girl's face as she shouted, "It's a bike!"

Goodness and patience rewarded; dreams fulfilled in sparkly pink perfection. The Clauses shared Gwen's unbridled bliss. "Santa brought me the bike I wanted!"

Steve had never imagined one toy could bring such joy. Santa looked at Arthur. The young man's face glowed as brightly as Gwen's.

Santa suddenly knew who had to be the next Santa—who had already become Santa. He turned gently to his older son and said, "Steve, you *deserve* to be Santa."

Steve had waited so long for this speech. Yet he could hardly believe the moment had arrived. His eyes filled at the thought that his father had finally acknowledged all his hard work! From his perfectly stitched pocket, he pulled out the tiny metal Santa from the board game.

Then Santa touched his arm and said, "But Steve . . . I wonder if Gwen is right."

Steve looked at Gwen, who squealed, "Can I have a go? Please, please, please?"

Steve realized that the girl's giddy laugh, her happy face, all of this was due to his "crazy" younger brother's "foolish" belief in Santa Claus. If it had been up to him, Gwen would still be waiting for a messenger to bring the present.

Steve understood. He held the Santa figure for just a moment longer before he handed it to Arthur and said, "I'll be the candle, eh?"

Arthur felt overwhelmed. He looked over to Grandsanta who raised both thumbs and whispered, "Whoopee!"

Santa looked at his sons and blinked his

watery eyes. "You're better men than me . . . both of you."

Gwen stopped crumpling the wrapping papers and exclaimed, "A bike . . . and a squirrel?! Ow!"

Having nipped the nipper on her finger, the startled squirrel raced out of the living room.

Bryony peeked in the window at the joyful scene and exclaimed, "Arthur, you did it!"

Likewise, the Mission Control elves celebrated the youngest Claus's triumph. On the big screen, the elves saw the three Santas emerge from Gwen's house, and the "gifts delivered" counter clicked from 000,000,001 down to all zeroes. Ernie shouted, "Drop complete!"

On their screen, the elves heard Bryony whisper, "Arthur is Santa!"

All the elves cheered, "Arthur! Arthur! Arthur!"

While Mrs. Claus dabbed tears of joy from her eyes, Steve and Santa were winched up to the S-1 holding grubby Grandsanta between them. The sooty old man hugged his pet reindeer as Dasher tried to lick the filth off his master's face.

With three Clauses and the remaining reindeer aboard, the winch went down once more to retrieve Arthur and the elf. Despite his magical new status, the young man was just as clumsy as ever.

Almost as soon as the rope lifted him, Arthur

banged into a tree and fell down on the snowy ground. When he stood up, a frosty white "beard" coated Arthur's chin. The wind puffed up his red parka, making him look like he had a big, round belly.

Just then Gwen glanced out the door; she saw what looked like something right off a Christmas card! The little girl could barely believe her eyes. Was it really . . . Santa Claus?

Then the squirrel raced out between her feet. When she looked up again, the wondrous vision was gone!

As Bryony and Arthur ascended into the S-1, they looked down at the little girl riding in happy circles on her new pink Twinkle Bike. Though the elf and the newest Santa would go on to share many merry holidays, both would always remember their first Christmas together as something quite out of this world.

Arthur works happily as a mail agent at the North Pole.

During the mission, Santa and an elf hide from a child who has woken!

Steve gives official orders from
Mission Control at the North Pole.

After successfully delivering the presents,
Santa triumphantly returns to the North Pole.

Oh no! Bryony explains
that a child was missed!

An excited Arthur discovers
the original sleigh, Eve.

Arthur is amazed as Grandsanta introduces the reindeer.

The descendents of the original eight reindeer wait for an adventure.

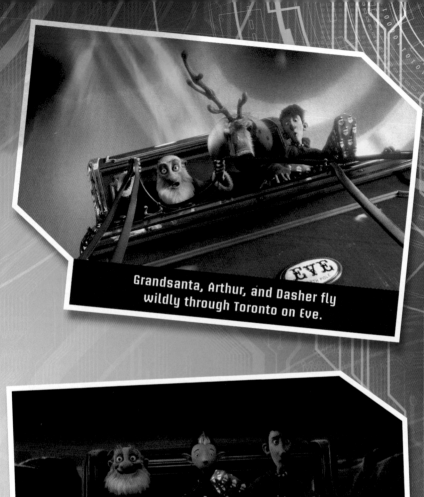

Grandsanta, Arthur, and Dasher fly
wildly through Toronto on Eve.

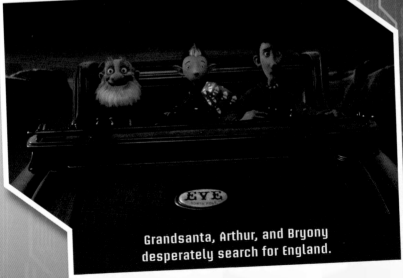

Grandsanta, Arthur, and Bryony
desperately search for England.

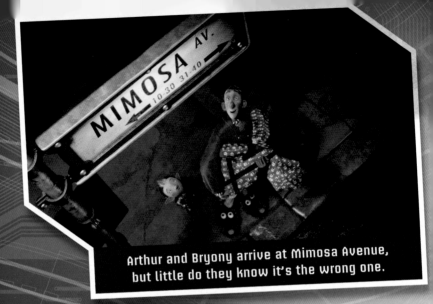

Arthur and Bryony arrive at Mimosa Avenue, but little do they know it's the wrong one.

At the end of his journey, Arthur successfully delivers the missed present and zips up to the S-1.

Behind the Scenes

The amazing art and dynamic animation for *Arthur Christmas* was not made overnight. It took artists years to perfect every last detail of the characters and environments. Before making it to the big screen, the talented teams at Aardman Animations and Sony Pictures Animation created hundreds of character and location sketches, sculptures, and paintings for inspiration. Their CG (computer-generated) experts then took that hand-drawn artwork and used it as a basis for the final film you see in theaters. Here is some "behind-the-scenes" art that shows how *Arthur Christmas* came to life!

Reference painting of the S-1.

Painting of Arthur and the original sleigh, Eve.

Development of Santa: sketch, sculpture, and final painting.

PINK TWINKLE BICYCLE

4778SBXK   [GWEN]

DELIVER TO:
4778SBXK
23 MIMOSA AVENUE
TREURU, CORNWALL, ENGLAND

FEATURES:

STREAMERS
SHINY BELL
FRONT/REAR BRAKE
SPARKLE PAINT
WHITE TIRES
SPARKLE PAINT STEEL FRAME
TRAINING WHEELS
REAR FENDER
SADDLE
CHAIN GAURD

STREAMERS
SPARKLE PAINT

SHINY BELL

WHITE TIRES

TRAINING WHEELS

Detailed graphic of Gwen and the bicycle.

Early sketch of Arthur working in his office.